9th April

Just—William

KT-386-002

Just—William

Richmal Crompton

First published in the U.K. in this new edition
in 1972 by William Collins Sons & Co. Ltd.,
London and Glasgow.
First published in Armada in 1974 by
William Collins Sons & Co. Ltd.,
14 St. James's Place, London SW1A 1PF

Printed in Great Britain by
Love & Malcomson Ltd., Brighton Road,
Redhill, Surrey.

Contents

The Publishers wish to make grateful acknowledgment to Richmal Crompton's niece, Richmal Ashbee, for her able assistance in editing this new edition of JUST—WILLIAM. Her knowledge and enthusiasm have been quite invaluable.

Introduction

William was eleven years old when his first book appeared in 1922 and happily, not being subject to the march of time, is still eleven years old in his last adventure —forty-six years later! When Richmal Crompton wrote her first "William" story—*The Outlaws*—in 1917, she had no thought of how William was to continue to tackle the problems of a changing world for over half a century; for though William has remained unaltered at eleven, the world around him has changed radically. He spent his early years in a large house with a big garden where the results of his ill-fated good intentions incurred the wrath of a succession of cooks, housemaids and gardeners. His older brother and sister, Robert and Ethel, seemed to pass their time in amateur dramatics and endless tennis parties. The cinema was in its infancy, and a bicycle was a young man's usual means of transport. Money, too, went a lot further than it does today, though never far enough for William's pressing day-to-day needs. The approach of war meant to him the excitement of Air Raid Precautions practice though the war itself brought big changes to the Brown family. First the servants, then Robert and Ethel left to help the War effort and William found himself helping his mother with the washing-up!

William is the "bad boy" of all the ages, but he isn't as black as he is painted. His insatiable curiosity may put the "fridge" out of action, immobilise the vacuum cleaner, fuse the electric lights, but it is the spirit of the inventor and the pioneer that inspires his work of destruction. He explores unknown stretches of country, plunging into ditches, climbing trees, doing battle with his enemies and comes home a sight to break a mother's heart, but his courage and initiative are the stuff of which heroes are made. He has sudden and spasmodic impulses to "help" his family. He "helps" wash up and leaves a trail of broken crockery in his wake; he "helps" get in the coal and covers hands, face and kitchen floor; he "helps" bring out the deck chairs and becomes inextricably entangled; he puts in a spot of gardening and no one can ever use the secateurs again. It is not always easy to remember how laudable his intentions are! But beneath his tough exterior, he is sensitive, generous and affectionate and despite his outrageous appearance and behaviour, he has a sense of dignity that you affront at your peril.

The extent of his success baffled his author. "I confess it is all a mystery. All I can suggest is that William must have some characteristic that is common to all human beings. Love of adventure? Inquisitiveness? Burning curiosity? Courage?"

William lost his chronicler when Richmal Crompton died in 1969, so there can be no record of how he is coping with the problems of the 70's. But that he is coping after his fashion, can we doubt? Does he not still pursue his reckless course in the fantasy world of our imagination? That William should cease is as unthinkable as that he should reach his twelfth birthday. Time stops for him and by the sheer force of his buoyant, thrusting personality he makes it stop for us too. May that grubby, tousled figure walk companionably with every generation of children to come. His creator would have wished it so.

CHAPTER I

WILLIAM GOES TO THE PICTURES

IT all began with William's aunt, who was in a good temper that Saturday morning and gave him a shilling for posting a letter for her and carrying her parcels from the grocer's.

"Buy some sweets or go to the pictures," she said carelessly, as she gave it to him.

William walked slowly down the road, gazing thoughtfully at the coin. After deep calculations, based on the fact that a shilling is the equivalent of two sixpences, he came to the conclusion that both luxuries could be indulged in. He could get into the stalls for sixpence and that left sixpence—more than enough, at the current cost of living, to keep him munching happily while he gazed at the screen.

In the matter of sweets, William frankly upheld the superiority of quantity over quality. Moreover, he knew every sweet shop within a two-mile radius of his home whose proprietor added an extra sweet after the scale had descended, and he patronised these shops exclusively. With solemn face and eager eye, he always watched the process of weighing, and "stingy" shops were known and banned by him.

He wandered now to his favourite confectioner and stood outside the window for five minutes, torn between the rival attractions of Gooseberry Eyes and Marble Balls. Both were sold at 4 ounces for 2d. William never purchased more expensive luxuries. At last his frowning brow relaxed and he entered the shop.

"Sixpennoth of Gooseberry Eyes," he said, with a slightly

self-conscious air. The extent of his purchases rarely exceeded a penny.

"Hello!" said the shopkeeper, in amused surprise.

"Gotter bit of money this mornin'," explained William carelessly, with the air of a Rothschild.

He watched the weighing of the emerald green dainties with silent intensity, saw with satisfaction the extra one added after the scale had fallen, received the precious paper bag and, putting two sweets into his mouth, walked out of the shop. Sucking slowly, he walked down the road towards the Picture Palace.

It was a thrilling programme. First came the story of desperate crooks who, on coming out of any building, glanced cautiously up and down the street in huddled, crouching attitudes, then crept ostentatiously on their way in a manner guaranteed to attract attention and suspicion at any place and time. The plot was involved. They were pursued by police, they leapt on to a moving train, and then, for no accountable reason, leapt from that on to a moving motor car, and from that they plunged into a moving river. It was thrilling, and William thrilled. Sitting quite motionless, he watched with wide, fascinated eyes, though his jaws never ceased their rotatory movement, and every now and then his hand would go mechanically to the paper bag on his knees and convey a Gooseberry Eye to his mouth.

The next film was a simple country love story, in which figured a simple country maiden wooed by the squire, who was marked out as the villain by his moustachios.

After many adventures the simple country maiden was won by a simple country son of the soil in picturesque rustic attire, whose emotions were faithfully portrayed by gestures that must have required much gymnastic skill; the villain was finally shown languishing in a prison cell, still indulging in frequent eyebrow play.

Next came another love story—this time of a noble-hearted couple, consumed with mutual passion and kept apart not only by a series of misunderstandings but also by maidenly pride and reserve on the part of the heroine and manly pride and reserve on the part of the hero that forced them to hide their ardour beneath a cold and haughty exterior. The heroine's brother moved through the story like a good fairy, tender and protective towards his orphan sister, and ultimately explained to each the burning passion of the other.

It was moving and touching and William was moved and touched.

The next was a comedy. It began with a solitary work-man engaged upon the re-painting of a door and ended with a miscellaneous crowd of people, all covered with paint, falling downstairs on top of one another. It was amusing. William was riotously and loudly amused.

Lastly came the pathetic story of a drunkard's downward path. He began as a wild young man in evening clothes drinking intoxicants and playing cards, he ended as a wild old man in rags still drinking intoxicants and playing cards. He had a small child with a pious and superior expression, who spent her time weeping over him and exhorting him to a better life, till, in a moment of justifiable exasperation, he threw a beer bottle at her head. He then bedewed her bed in hospital with penitent tears, tore out his hair, flung up his arms towards heaven, beat his waistcoat, and clasped her to his breast, so that it was not to be wondered at that, after all that excitement, the child had a relapse and, with the words "Good-bye, Father. Do not think of what you have done. I forgive you," passed peacefully away.

William drew a deep breath at the end and, still sucking, arose with the throng and filed out.

Once outside, he glanced cautiously around and slunk down the road in the direction of his home. Then he doubled suddenly and ran down a back street to put his imaginary pursuers off his track. He took a pencil from his pocket and, levelling it at the empty air, fired twice. Two of his pursuers fell dead, the rest came on with redoubled vigour. There was no time to be lost. Running for dear life, he dashed down the next street, leaving in his wake an elderly gentleman nursing his toe and cursing volubly. As he neared his gate, William again drew his pencil from his pocket and, still looking back down the road and firing as he went, rushed into his own gateway.

William's father, who had stayed at home that day because of a bad headache and a touch of liver trouble, picked himself up from the middle of a rhododendron bush and seized William by the back of his neck.

"You young ruffian," he roared, "what do you mean by charging into me like that?"

William gently disengaged himself.

"I wasn't chargin', Father," he said meekly. "I was only jus' comin' in at the gate, same as other folks. I jus' wasn't looking jus' the way you were coming, but I can't look all ways at once, 'cause—"

"Be *quiet*!" roared William's father.

Like the rest of the family, he dreaded William's eloquence.

"What's that on your tongue? Put your tongue out."

William obeyed. The colour of William's tongue would have put to shame Spring's freshest tints.

"How many times must I tell you," bellowed William's father, "that I won't have you going about eating filthy poisons all day between meals?"

"It's not filthy poison," said William. "It's jus' a few sweets Aunt Susan gave me 'cause I kin'ly went to the post office for her an'—"

"Be *quiet*! Have you got any more of the foul things?"

"They're not foul things," said William doggedly. "They're good. Jus' have one an' try. They're jus' a few sweets Aunt Susan kin'ly gave me an'—"

"Be *quiet*! Where are they?"

Slowly and reluctantly William drew forth his bag. His father seized it and flung it far into the bushes. For the next ten minutes William conducted a thorough and systematic

14

search among the bushes and for the rest of the day consumed Gooseberry Eyes and garden soil in fairly equal proportions.

He wandered round to the back garden and climbed on to the wall.

"Hello!" said the little girl next door, looking up.

Something about the little girl's head and curls reminded William of the simple country maiden. There was a touch of the artistic temperament about William. He promptly felt himself the simple country son of the soil.

"Hullo, Joan," he said in a deep, husky voice, intended to be expressive of intense affection. "Have you missed me while I've been away?"

"Didn't know you'd been away," said Joan. "What are you talking so funny for?"

"I'm not talkin' funny," said William in the same husky voice. "I can't help talkin' like this."

"You've got a cold. That's what you've got. That's what Mother said when she saw you splashing about with your rain tub this morning. She said, 'The next thing that we shall hear of William Brown will be he's in bed with a cold.'"

"It's not a cold," said William mysteriously. "It's jus' the way I feel."

"What are you eating?"

"Gooseberry Eyes. Like one?" He took the packet from his pocket and handed it down to her. "Go on. Take two—three," he said in reckless generosity.

"But they're—dirty."

"Go on. It's only ord'nary dirt. It soon sucks off. They're jolly good." He poured a shower of them lavishly down to her.

"I say," he said, reverting to his character of simple country lover. "Did you say you'd missed me? I bet you didn't think of me as much as I did of you. I jus' bet you didn't." His voice had sunk deeper and deeper till it almost died away.

"I say, William, does your throat hurt you awful, that you've got to talk like that?"

Her blue eyes were anxious and sympathetic.

William put one hand to his throat and frowned.

"A bit," he confessed lightly.

"Oh, William!" she clasped her hands. "Does it hurt all the time?"

Her solicitude was flattering.

"I don't talk much about it, anyway, do I?" he said manfully.

She started up and stared at him with big blue eyes.

"Oh, William! Is it—is it your—lungs? I've got an aunt that's got lungs and she coughs and coughs," William coughed hastily, "and it hurts her and makes her awful bad. Oh, William, I do *hope* you've not got lungs."

Her tender, anxious little face was upturned to him. "I guess I have got lungs," he said, "but I don't make a fuss about 'em."

He coughed again.

"What does the doctor say about it?"

William considered a minute.

"He says it's lungs all right," he said at last. "He says I gotter be jolly careful."

"William, would you like my new paintbox?"

"I don't think so. Not now. Thanks."

"I've got three balls and one's quite new. Wouldn't you like it, William?"

"No—thanks. You see, it's no use my collectin' a lot of things. You never know—with lungs."

"Oh, *William!*"

Her distress was pathetic.

"Of course," he said hastily, "if I'm careful it'll be all right. Don't you worry about me."

"Joan!" from the house.

"That's Mother. Good-bye, William, dear. If Father brings me home any chocolate, I'll bring it in to you. I will —honest. Thanks for the Gooseberry Eyes. Good-bye."

"Good-bye—and don't worry about me," he added bravely.

He put another Gooseberry Eye into his mouth and wandered round aimlessly to the front of the house. His elder sister Ethel was at the front door, shaking hands with a young man.

"I'll do all I can for you," she was saying earnestly.

Their hands were clasped.

"I know you will," he said, equally earnestly.

Both look and handclasp were long. The young man walked away. Ethel stood at the door, gazing after him, with a far-away look in her eyes. William was interested.

"That was Jack Morgan, wasn't it?" he said.

"Yes," said Ethel absently, and went into the house.

The look, the long handclasp, the words lingered in William's memory. They must be jolly fond of each other, like people are when they're engaged, but he knew they weren't engaged. P'raps they were too proud to let each other know how fond they were of each other—like the man and girl in the film. Ethel wanted a brother like the one in the film to let the man know she was fond of him. Then a light came suddenly into William's mind and he stood, deep in thought.

Inside the drawing-room, Ethel was talking to her mother.

"He's going to propose to her next Sunday. He told me about it because I'm her best friend, and he wanted to ask me if I thought he'd any chance. I said I thought he had, and I said I'd try and prepare her a little and put in a good word for him if I could. Isn't it thrilling?"

"Yes, dear. By the way, did you see William anywhere? I do hope he's not in mischief."

"He was in the front garden a minute ago." She went to the window. "He's not there now, though."

William had just arrived at Mr. Morgan's house.

The maid showed him into Mr. Morgan's sitting-room.

"Mr. Brown," she announced.

The young man rose to receive his guest with politeness

not unmixed with bewilderment. His acquaintance with William was of the slightest.

"Good afternoon," said William. "I've come from Ethel."

"Yes?"

"Yes." William fumbled in his pocket and at last drew forth a rosebud, slightly crushed by its close confinement in the company of the Gooseberry Eyes, a penknife, a top, and a piece of putty.

"She sent you this," said William gravely.

Mr. Morgan gazed at it with the air of one who is sleep-walking.

"Yes? Er—very kind of her."

"Kinder keep-sake. Souvenir," explained William.

"Yes. Er—any message?"

"Oh, yes. She wants you to come in and see her this evening."

"Er—yes. Of course. I've just come from her. Perhaps she remembered something she wanted to tell me after I'd gone."

"P'raps."

Then, "Any particular time?"

"No. 'Bout seven, I expect."

"Oh, yes."

Mr. Morgan's eyes were fixed with a fascinated wondering gaze upon the limp, and by no means spotless, rosebud.

"You say she—sent this?"

"Yes."

"And no other message?"

"No."

"Er—well, say I'll come with pleasure, will you?"

"Yes."

Silence.

Then, "She thinks an awful lot of you, Ethel does."

Mr. Morgan passed a hand over his brow.

"Yes? Kind—er—very kind, I'm sure."

"Always talkin' about you in her sleep," went on

18

William, warming to his theme. "I sleep in the next room and I can hear her talkin' about you all night. Jus' sayin' your name over and over again. 'Jack Morgan, Jack Morgan, Jack Morgan.' " William's voice was husky and soulful. "Jus' like that—over an' over again. 'Jack Morgan, Jack Morgan, Jack Morgan.' "

Mr. Morgan was speechless. He sat gazing with horror-stricken face at his young visitor.

"Are you—*sure*?" he said at last. "It might be someone else's name."

"No, 'tisn't," said William firmly. "It's yours. 'Jack Morgan, Jack Morgan, Jack Morgan'—jus' like that. An' she eats just nothin' now. Always hangin' round the windows to watch you pass."

The perspiration stood out in beads on Mr. Morgan's brow.

"It's—*horrible*," he said at last, in a hoarse whisper.

William was gratified. The young man had at last realised his cruelty. But William never liked to leave a task half done. He still sat on and calmly and silently considered his next statement. Mechanically he put a hand into his pocket and conveyed a Gooseberry Eye to his mouth. Mr. Morgan also sat in silence with a stricken look upon his face, gazing into vacancy.

"She's got your photo," said William at last, "fixed up into one of those little round things on a chain round her neck."

"Are—you—sure?" said Mr. Morgan desperately.

"Sure's fate," said William, rising. "Well, I'd better be goin'. She pertic-ler wants to see you alone to-night. Good-bye."

But Mr. Morgan did not answer. He sat huddled up in his chair staring in front of him long after William had gone jauntily on his way. Then he moistened his dry lips.

"Good Lord," he groaned.

William was thinking of the films as he went home. That painter one was jolly good. When they all got paint all over!

19

And when they all fell downstairs! William suddenly guffawed out loud at the memory. But what had the painter chap been doing at the very beginning before he began to paint? He'd been getting off the old paint with a sort of torch thing and a knife, then he began putting the new paint on. Just sort of melting the old paint and then scraping it off. William had never seen it done in real life, but he supposed that was the way you did get old paint off. Melting it with some sort of fire, then scraping it off. He wasn't sure whether it was that, but he could find out. As he entered the house he took his penknife from his pocket, opened it thoughtfully, and went upstairs.

Mr. Brown came home about dinner-time.

"How's your head, Father?" said Ethel sympathetically.

"Rotten!" said Mr. Brown, sinking wearily into an arm-chair.

"Perhaps dinner will do it good," said Mrs. Brown. "It ought to be ready now."

The housemaid entered the room.

"Mr. Morgan, Mum. He wants to see Miss Ethel. I've shown him into the dining-room."

"*Now?*" exploded Mr. Brown. "What the deu—why the dickens is the young idiot coming at this time of day? Seven o'clock! What time does he think we have dinner? What does he mean by coming round paying calls on people at dinner-time? What—"

"Ethel, dear," interrupted Mrs. Brown, "do go and see what he wants and get rid of him as soon as you can."

Ethel entered the dining-room, carefully closing the door behind her to keep out the sound of her father's comments, which were plainly audible across the hall.

She noticed a wan and haggard look on Mr. Morgan's face as he rose to greet her.

"Er—good evening, Miss Brown."

"Good evening, Mr. Morgan."

Then they sat in silence, both awaiting some explanation of the visit. The silence became oppressive. Mr. Morgan, with an air of acute misery and embarrassment, shifted his feet and coughed. Ethel looked at the clock. Then—

"Was it raining when you came, Mr. Morgan?"

"Raining? Er—no. No—not at all."

Silence.

"I thought it looked like rain this afternoon."

"Yes, of course. Er—no, not at all."

Silence.

"It does make the roads so bad round here when it rains."

"Yes." Mr. Morgan put up a hand as though to loosen his collar. "Er—very bad."

"Almost impassable."

"Er—quite."

Silence again.

Inside the drawing-room, Mr. Brown was growing restive.

"Is dinner to be kept waiting for that youth all night? Quarter-past seven! You know it's just what I can't stand—having my meals interfered with. Is my digestion to be ruined simply because this young nincompoop chooses to pay his social calls at seven o'clock at night?"

"Then we must ask him to dinner," said Mrs. Brown, desperately. "We really must."

"We must *not*," said Mr. Brown. "Can't I stay away from the office for one day with a headache, without having to entertain all the young jackasses for miles around." The telephone bell rang. He raised his hands above his head. "Oh—"

"I'll go, dear," said Mrs. Brown hastily.

She returned with a worried frown on her brow.

"It's Mrs. Clive," she said. "She says Joan has been very sick because of some horrible sweets William gave her, and she said she was so sorry to hear about William and hoped he'd be better soon. I couldn't quite make it out, but it seems that William has been telling them that he had to go and see a doctor about his lungs and the doctor said they

21

were very weak and he'd have to be careful."

Mr. Brown sat up and looked at her. "But—why—on—earth?" he said slowly.

"I don't know, dear," said Mrs. Brown helplessly. "I don't know anything about it."

"He's mad," said Mr. Brown with conviction. "Mad. It's the only explanation."

Then came the opening and shutting of the front door and Ethel entered. She was very flushed.

"He's gone," she said. "Mother, it's simply horrible! He didn't tell me much, but it seems that William actually went to his house and told him that I wanted to see him alone at seven o'clock this evening. I've hardly spoken to William to-day. He couldn't have misunderstood anything I said. And he actually took a flower with him—a dreadful-looking rosebud—and said I'd sent it. I simply didn't know where to look or what to say. It was horrible!"

Mrs. Brown sat gazing weakly at her daughter.

Mr. Brown rose with the air of a man goaded beyond endurance.

"Where *is* William!" he said shortly.

"I don't know, but I thought I heard him go upstairs some time ago."

William *was* upstairs. For the last twenty minutes he had been happily and quietly engaged upon his bedroom door with a lighted taper in one hand and penknife in the other. There was no doubt about it. By successful experiment he had proved that that was the way you got old paint off. When Mr. Brown came upstairs he had entirely stripped one panel of its paint.

An hour later William sat in the back garden on an up-turned box sucking, with a certain dogged defiance, the last and dirtiest of the Gooseberry Eyes. Sadly he reviewed the day. It had not been a success. His generosity to the little girl next door had been misconstrued into an attempt upon her life, his efforts to help on his only sister's love affair had been painfully misunderstood, and lastly, because (among other things) he had discovered a perfectly scientific method of removing old paint, he had been brutally assaulted by a violent and unreasonable parent. Suddenly William began to wonder if his father drank. He saw himself, through a mist of pathos, as a drunkard's child. He tried to imagine his father weeping over him in hospital and begging his forgiveness. It was a wonder he wasn't there now, anyway. His shoulders drooped—his whole attitude became expressive of extreme dejection.

Inside the house his father, reclining at length in an armchair, discoursed to his wife on the subject of his son. One hand was pressed to his aching brow, and the other gesticulating freely. "He's insane," he said, "stark, raving insane. You ought to take him to a doctor and get his brain examined. Look at him to-day. He begins by knocking me into the middle of the rhododendron bushes—under no provocation, mind you. I hadn't spoken to him. Then he tries to poison that nice little thing next door with some vile stuff I thought I'd thrown away. Then he goes about telling people he's consumptive. He looks it, doesn't he? Then he takes extraordinary messages and love tokens from Ethel to strange young men and brings them here just when we're going to begin dinner, and then goes round burning and hacking at the doors. Where's the sense in it—in any of it? They're the acts of a lunatic—you ought to have his brain examined."

Mrs. Brown cut off her darning wool and laid aside the sock she had just finished darning.

"It certainly sounds very silly, dear," she said mildly. "But there might be some explanation of it all, if only we knew. Boys are such funny things."

She looked at the clock and went over to the window. "William!" she called. "It's your bedtime, dear."

William rose sadly and came slowly into the house.

"Good night, Mother," he said; then he turned a mournful and reproachful eye upon his father.

"Good night, Father," he said. "Don't think about what you've done, I for—"

He stopped, and decided, hastily but wisely, to retire with all possible speed.

CHAPTER 2

WILLIAM THE INTRUDER

"SHE'S different from everybody else in the world," stammered Robert ecstatically. "You simply couldn't describe her. No one could!"

His mother continued to darn his socks and made no comment.

Only William, his young brother, showed interest.

"*How's* she different from anyone else?" he demanded. "Has she got two heads or sumthin'?"

Robert turned on him with exasperation.

"Oh, go and play at trains!" he said. "A child like you can't understand anything."

William retired with dignity to the window and listened, with interest unabated, to the rest of the conversation.

"Yes, but who is she, dear?" said their mother. "Robert, I can't *think* how you get these big holes in your heels!"

Robert ran his hands wildly through his hair.

"I've *told* you who she is, Mother," he said. "I've been talking about her ever since I came into the room."

"Yes, I know, dear, but you haven't mentioned her name or anything about her."

"Well," Robert spoke with an air of super-human patience, "she's a Miss Cannon and she's staying with the Clives and I met her out with Mrs. Clive this morning and she introduced me and she's the most beautiful girl I've ever seen and she—"

"Yes," said Mrs. Brown hastily, "you told me all that."

"Well," went on the infatuated Robert, "we must have

her to tea. I know I can't marry yet—not while I'm still at college—but I could get to know her. Not that I suppose she'd look at me. She's miles above me—miles above anyone. She's the most beautiful girl I've ever seen. You can't imagine her. You wouldn't believe me if I described her. No one could describe her. She—"

Mrs. Brown interrupted him with haste.

"I'll ask Mrs. Clive to bring her over one afternoon. I've no more of this blue wool, Robert. I wish you didn't have your socks such different colours. I shall have to use mauve. It's right on the heel; it won't show."

Robert gave a gasp of horror.

"You *can't*, Mother. How do you know it won't show? And even if it didn't show, the thought of it—! It's—it's a crisis of my life now I've met her. I can't go about feeling ridiculous."

"I say," said William open-mouthed. "Are you spoony on her?"

"William, don't use such vulgar expressions," said Mrs. Brown. "Robert just feels a friendly interest in her, don't you, Robert?"

"A 'friendly interest'!" groaned Robert in despair. "No one ever *tries* to understand what I feel. After all I've told you about her and that she's the most beautiful girl I've ever seen and miles above me and above anyone and you think I feel a 'friendly interest' in her. It's—it's the one great passion of my life! It's—"

"Well," put in Mrs. Brown mildly, "I'll ring up Mrs. Clive and ask if she's doing anything to-morrow afternoon."

Robert's tragic young face lit up, then he stood wrapt in thought, and a cloud of anxiety overcast it.

"Ellen can press the trousers of my brown suit to-night, can't she? And, Mother, could you get me some socks and a tie before to-morrow? Blue, I think—a bright blue, you know, not too bright, but not so as you don't notice them. I wish the laundry was a decent one. You know, a man's collar ought to *shine* when it's new on. They never put a

26

shine on to them. I'd better have some new ones for to-morrow. It's so important, how one looks. She—people *judge* you on how you look. They—"

Mrs. Brown laid her work aside.

"I'll go and ring up Mrs. Clive now," she said.

When she returned, William had gone and Robert was standing by the window, his face pale with suspense, and a Napoleonic frown on his brow.

"Mrs. Clive can't come," announced Mrs. Brown in her comfortable voice, "but Miss Cannon will come alone. It appears she's met Ethel before. So you needn't worry any more, dear."

Robert gave a sardonic laugh.

"*Worry!*" he said. "There's plenty to worry about still. What about William?"

"Well, what about him?"

"Well, can't he go away somewhere to-morrow? Things never go right when William's there. You know they don't."

"The poor boy must have tea with us, dear. He'll be very good, I'm sure. Ethel will be home then and she'll help. I'll tell William not to worry you. I'm sure he'll be good."

William had received specific instructions. He was not to come into the house till the tea-bell rang, and he was to go out and play in the garden again directly after tea. He was perfectly willing to obey them. He was thrilled by the thought of Robert in the role of the lovelorn hero. He took the situation quite seriously.

He was in the garden when the visitor came up the drive. He had been told not to obtrude himself upon her notice, so he crept up silently and peered at her through the rhodo-dendron bushes. The proceeding also happened to suit his character of the moment, which was that of a Red Indian chief.

Miss Cannon was certainly pretty. She had brown hair, brown eyes, and dimples that came and went. She walked

27

up the drive, looking neither to right nor left, till a slight movement in the bushes arrested her attention. She turned quickly and saw a small boy's face, smeared black with burnt cork and framed in hens' feathers held on with tape. The dimples peeped out.

"Hail, O great chief!" she said.

William gazed at her open-mouthed. Such intelligence on the part of a grown-up was unusual.

"Chief Red Hand!" he supplied with a fierce scowl.

She bowed low, brown eyes alight with merriment.

"And what death awaits the poor white face who has fallen defenceless into his hand?"

"You better come quiet to my wigwam an' see," said Red Hand darkly.

She threw a glance to the bend in the drive behind which lay the house, and with a low laugh followed him through the bushes. From one point the drawing-room window could be seen, and there the anxious Robert stood, pale with anxiety, stiff and upright in his newly-creased trousers, his soulful eyes fixed steadfastly on the bend in the drive round which the beloved should come. Every now and then his nervous hand wandered up to touch the new tie and gleaming new collar, which was rather too high and too tight for comfort, but which the shopkeeper had informed his harassed customer was the "latest and most correct shape".

Meanwhile the beloved had reached William's "dug-out." William had made this himself of branches cut down from the trees and spent many happy hours in it with one or other of his friends.

"Here is the wigwam, Pale-face," he said in a sepulchral voice. "Stand here while I decide with Snake Face and the other chiefs what's goin' to be done to you. There's Snake Face an' the others," he added in his natural voice, pointing to a small cluster of shrubs.

Approaching these, he stood and talked fiercely and unintelligibly for a few minutes, turning his scowling corked face and pointing his finger at her every now and then as, apparently, he described his captive.

Then he approached her again.

"That was Red Indian what I was talkin' then," he explained in his ordinary voice, then sinking it to its low, roaring note and scowling more ferociously than ever, "Snake Face says the Pale-face must be scalped and cooked and eat!"

He took out a penknife and opened it as though to perform the operation, then continued, "But me and the others say that if you'll be a squaw an' cook for us we'll let you go alive."

Miss Cannon dropped on to her knees.

"Most humble and grateful thanks, great Red Hand," she said. "I will with pleasure be your squaw."

"I've gotter fire round here," said William proudly, leading her to the back of the wigwam, where a small wood fire smouldered spiritlessly, choked by a large tin full of dark liquid.

"That, O Squaw," said Red Hand with a dramatic gesture, "is a Pale-face we caught las' night!"

The squaw clasped her hands together.

"Oh, how *lovely*!" she said. "Is he cooking?"

Red Hand nodded. Then—

"I'll get you some feathers," he said obligingly. "You oughter have feathers too."

He retired into the depths of the wigwam and returned with a handful of hen feathers. Miss Cannon stuck the feathers into her fluffy brown hair with a laugh.

"This is jolly!" she said. "I love Red Indians!"

"I've got some cork you can have to do your face too," went on William with reckless generosity. "It soon burns in the fire."

She threw a glance towards the chimneys of the house that could be seen through the trees and shook her pretty head regretfully.

"I'm afraid I'd better not," she said sadly.

"Well," he said, "now I'll go huntin' and you stir the Pale-face and we'll eat him when I come back. Now, I'll be off. You watch me track."

He opened his clasp-knife with a bloodthirsty flourish and, casting sinister glances round him, crept upon his hands and knees into the bushes. He circled about, well within his squaw's vision, obviously bent upon impressing her. She stirred the mixture in the tin with a twig and threw him every now and then the admiring glances he so evidently desired.

Soon he returned, carrying over his shoulder a doormat which he threw down at her feet.

"A venison, O Squaw," he said in a lordly voice. "Let it be cooked. I've had it out all morning," he added in his ordinary tones; "they've not missed it yet."

He fetched from the "wigwam" two small jagged tins and, taking the larger tin off the fire, poured some into each.

"Now," he said, "here's some Pale-face for you, squaw."

"Oh," she said, "I'm sure he's awfully good, but—"

"You needn't be frightened of it," said William protectively. "It's jolly good, I can tell you." He picked up the cover of a packet of soup from behind the trees. "It's jus' that and water and it's jolly good!"

"How lovely! Do they let you—?"

"They don't let me," he broke in hastily, "but there's heaps in the larder and they don't notice one every now an' then. Go on!" he said encouragingly, "I don't mind you having it! Honest, I don't! I'll get some more soon."

Bravely she raised the tin to her lips and took a sip.

"Gorgeous!" she said, shutting her eyes. Then she drained the tin.

William's face shone with pride and happiness. But it clouded over as the sound of a bell rang out from the house.

"Crumbs! That's tea!"

Hastily Miss Cannon took the feathers from her hair.

"You don't keep a looking-glass in your wigwam, I suppose?" she said.

30

"N-no," admitted William. "But I'll get one for next time you come. I'll get one from Ethel's room."

"Won't she mind?"

"She won't know," said William simply.

Miss Cannon smoothed down her dress.

"I'm horribly late. What will they think of me? It was awful of me to come with you. I'm always doing awful things. That's a secret between you and me." She gave William a smile that dazzled him. "Now come in and we'll confess."

"I can't," said William. "I've got to wash an' come down tidy. I promised I would. It's a special day. Because of Robert, you know. Well, *you* know. Because of—Robert!"

He looked up at her mystified face with a significant nod.

Robert was frantic. He had run his hands through his hair so often that it stood around his head like a spiked halo.

"We *can't* begin without her," he said. "She'll think we're awful. It will—put her off me for ever. She's not used to being treated like that. She's the sort of girl people don't begin without. She's the most beautiful girl I've ever met in all my life and you—my own mother—treat her like this. You may be ruining my life. You've no idea what this means to me. If you'd seen her you'd feel more sympathy. I simply can't describe her—I—"

"I said four o'clock, Robert," said Mrs. Brown firmly, "and it's after half-past. Ethel, tell Emma she can ring the bell and bring in tea."

The perspiration stood out on Robert's brow.

"It's—the downfall of all my hopes," he said hoarsely.

Then, a few minutes after the echoes of the tea-bell died away, the front door bell rang sharply. Robert stroked his hair down with wild, unrestrained movements of his hands, and summoned a tortured smile to his lips.

Miss Cannon appeared upon the threshold, bewitching and demure.

"Aren't I perfectly disgraceful?" she said with her low laugh. "To tell the truth, I met your little boy in the drive and I've been with him some time. He's a perfect little dear, isn't he?"

Her brown eyes rested on Robert. He moistened his lips and smiled his tortured smile, but was beyond speech.

"Yes, I know Ethel, and I met your son—*yesterday*, wasn't it?"

Robert murmured unintelligibly, raising one hand to the too tight collar, and then bowed vaguely in her direction.

Then they went in to tea.

William, his hair well brushed, the cork partially washed from his face, and the feathers removed, arrived a few minutes later. Conversation was carried on chiefly by Miss Cannon and Ethel. Robert racked his brain for some striking remark, something that would raise him in her esteem far above the ranks of ordinary young men, but nothing came. Whenever her brown eyes rested on him, however, he summoned the mirthless smile to his lips and raised a hand to relieve the strain of the imprisoning collar. Desperately he felt the precious moments passing and his passion yet unrevealed, except by his eyes, whose message he was afraid she had not read.

As they rose from tea, William turned to his mother, with an anxious sibilant whisper.

"Ought *I* to have put on my best suit *too*?"

Amusement danced in Miss Cannon's eyes, and the look the perspiring Robert sent him would have crushed a less bold spirit.

William had quite forgotten the orders he had received to retire from the scene directly after tea. He was impervious to all hints. He followed in the train of the all-conquering Miss Cannon to the drawing-room and sat on the sofa with Robert, who had taken his seat next to his beloved.

"Are you—er—fond of reading, Miss Cannon?" began Robert with a painful effort.

"I—*wrote* a story once," said William boastfully, leaning

over Robert before she could answer. "It was a jolly good one. I showed it to some people. I'll show it to you if you like. It began with a pirate on a raft an' he'd stole some jewel'ry and the king the jewels belonged to was coming after him on a steamer and jus' when he was comin' up to him he jumped into the water and took the jewls with him an' a fish eat the jewels and the king caught it an' "—he paused for breath.

"I'd love to read it!" said Miss Cannon.

Robert turned sideways, and resting an arm on his knee to exclude the persistent William, spoke in a husky voice.

"What is your favourite flower, Miss Cannon?"

William's small head was craned round Robert's arm.

"I've gotter garden. I've got Virginia Stock grow'n all over it. It grows up in no time. An' must'erd 'n cress grows in no time too. I like things what grow quick, don't you? You get tired of waiting for the other sorts, don't you?"

Robert rose desperately.

"Would you care to see the garden and greenhouses, Miss Cannon?" he said.

"I'd love to," said Miss Cannon.

With a threatening glare at William, Robert led the way to the garden. And William, all innocent animation, followed.

"Can you tie knots what can't come untied?" he demanded.

"No," she said, "I wish I could."

"I can. I'll show you. I'll get a piece of string and show you afterwards. It's easy but it wants practice, that's all. An' I'll teach you how to make aeroplanes out of paper what fly in the air when it's windy. That's quite easy. Only you've gotter be careful to get 'em the right size. I can make 'em and I can make lots of things out of matchboxes an' things an'—"

The infuriated Robert interrupted.

"These are my father's roses. He's very proud of them."

"They're beautiful."

"Well, wait till you see my Virginia Stock, that's all. Wait—"

"Will you have this tea-rose, Miss Cannon?" Robert's face was purple as he presented it. "It—it—er—it suits you. You—er—flowers and you—that is—I'm sure—you love flowers—you should—er—always have flowers. If I—"

"An' I'll get you those red ones and that white one," broke in the equally infatuated William, determined not to be outshone. "An' I'll get you some of my Virginia Stock. An' I don't give my Virginia Stock to *anyone*," he added with emphasis.

When they re-entered the drawing-room, Miss Cannon carried a large bouquet of Virginia Stock and white and red roses which completely hid Robert's tea-rose. William was by her side, chatting airily and confidently. Robert followed—a pale statue of despair.

In answer to Robert's agonised glance, Mrs. Brown summoned William to her corner, while Robert and Miss Cannon took their seats again upon the sofa.

"I hope—I hope," said Robert soulfully, "I hope your stay here is a long one?"

"Well, why can't I jus' *speak* to her?" William's whisper was loud and indignant.

" 'Sh, dear!" said Mrs. Brown.

"I should like to show you some of the walks around here," went on Robert desperately with a fearful glance towards the corner where William stood in righteous indignation before his mother. "If I could have that—er—pleasure—er—honour?"

"I was only jus' *speaking* to her," went on William's voice. "I wasn't doin' any harm, was I? Only *speaking* to her!"

The silence was intense. Robert, purple, opened his lips to say something, anything to drown that horrible voice, but nothing would come. Miss Cannon was obviously listening to William.

"Is no one else ever to *speak* to her"—the sibilant whisper, raised in indignant appeal, filled all the room—

"jus' 'cause Robert's fell in love with her?"

The horror of the moment haunted Robert's nights and days for weeks to come.

Mrs. Brown coughed hastily and began to describe at unnecessary length the ravages of the caterpillars upon her husband's favourite rose-tree.

William withdrew with dignity to the garden and a minute later Miss Cannon rose from the sofa.

"I must be going, I'm afraid," she said with a smile.

Robert, anguished and overpowered, rose slowly.

"You must come again some time," he said weakly, but with passion undaunted.

"I will," she said. "I'm longing to see more of William. I adore William!"

They comforted Robert's wounded feelings as best they could, but it was Ethel who devised the plan that finally cheered him. She suggested a picnic on the following Thursday, which happened to be Robert's birthday, and incidentally the last day of Miss Cannon's visit, and the picnic-party was to consist of—Robert, Ethel, Mrs. Clive and Miss Cannon, and William was not even to be told where it was to be. The invitation was sent that evening and Robert spent the week dreaming of picnic lunches and suggesting impossible dainties of which the cook had never heard. It was not until she threatened to give notice that he reluctantly agreed to leave the arrangements to her. He sent his white flannels (which were perfectly clean) to the laundry with a note attached, hinting darkly at legal proceedings if they were not sent back, spotless, by Thursday morning. He went about with an expression of set and solemn purpose upon his frowning countenance. William he utterly ignored. He bought a book of poems at a second-hand bookshop and kept them on the table by his bed.

They saw nothing of Miss Cannon in the interval, but Thursday dawned bright and clear, and Robert's anxious spirits rose. He was presented with a new bicycle by his father, a watch by his mother, and a tin of toffee (given not without ulterior motive) by William.

They met Mrs. Clive and Miss Cannon at the station and took tickets to a village a few miles away whence they had decided to walk to a shady spot on the river bank.

William's dignity was slightly offended by his pointed exclusion from the party, but he had resigned himself to it and spent the first part of the morning in the character of Chief Red Hand among the rhododendron bushes. He had added an ostrich feather found in the boxroom to his head-dress, and used almost a whole cork on his face. He wore the doormat pinned to his shoulders.

After melting some treacle toffee in rain-water over his smoking fire, adding orange juice and drinking the resulting liquid, he tired of the game and wandered upstairs to Robert's bedroom to inspect his birthday presents. The tin of toffee was on the table by Robert's bed. William took one or two as a matter of course and began to read the love-poems. He was horrified a few minutes later to see the tin empty, but he fastened the lid with a sigh, wondering if Robert would guess who had eaten them. He was afraid he would. Anyway, he'd given him them. And anyway, he hadn't known he was eating them.

He then went to the dressing-table and tried on the watch, but resisted the temptation to wear it for the rest of the morning and replaced it on the dressing-table.

Then he wandered downstairs and round to the shed, where Robert's new bicycle stood in all its glory. It was shining and spotless and William gazed at it in awe and admiration. He came to the conclusion that he could do it no possible harm by leading it carefully round the house. Encouraged by the fact that Mrs. Brown was out shopping, he walked it round the house several times. He much enjoyed the feeling of importance and possession that it gave him. He felt loath to part with it. He wondered if it was very hard to ride. He had never tried a full-size two-wheeler. He stood on a garden bench and with difficulty transferred himself from that to the bicycle seat. To his surprise and delight he rode for a few yards before he fell off. He tried again and fell off again. He tried again and rode straight into a holly bush. He forgot everything in his determination to master the art. He tried again and again. He fell off or rode into the holly bush again and again. The shining black paint of the bicycle was scratched, the handle-bars were slightly bent and dulled; William himself was bruised and battered but unbeaten.

At last he managed to avoid the fatal magnet of the holly bush, to steer an unsteady zig-zag course down the drive and out into the road. He had had no particular intention of riding into the road. In fact, he was still wearing his be-feathered headgear, blacked face, and the mat pinned to his shoulders. It was only when he was actually in the road that he realised that retreat was impossible, that he had no idea how to get off the bicycle.

What followed was to William more like a nightmare than anything else. He saw a lorry coming towards him and in sudden panic turned down a side-street, and from that into another side-street. People came out of their houses to watch him pass. Children booed or cheered him and ran after him in crowds. And William went on and on simply because he could not stop. His iron nerve had failed him. He had not even the presence of mind to fall off. He was quite lost. He had left the town behind him and did not know where he was going. But wherever he went he was the centre of attraction. The strange figure with blackened, streaked face, mat flying behind in the wind, and a head-dress of feathers from which every now and then one floated away, brought the population to its doors. Some said he had escaped from an asylum, some that he was an advertisement for something. The children were inclined to think he was part of a circus. William himself had passed beyond despair. His first panic had changed to a dull certainty that this would go on for ever. He would never know how to stop. He supposed he would go right across England. He wondered if he were near the sea now. He couldn't be far off. He wondered if he would ever see his mother and father again. And his feet pedalled mechanically along. They did not reach the pedals at their lowest point; they had to catch them as they came up and send them down with all their might.

It was very tiring. William wondered if people would be sorry if he dropped down dead.

I have said that William did not know where he was going.

But Fate knew.

The picnickers walked down the hill from the little station to the river bank. It was a beautiful morning. Robert, his heart and hopes high, walked beside his goddess, revelling in his nearness to her though he could think of nothing to say to her. But Ethel and Mrs. Clive chattered gaily.

"We've given William the slip," said Ethel with a laugh. "He's no idea where we've gone even!"

"I'm sorry," said Miss Cannon. "I'd have loved William to be here."

"You don't know him," said Ethel fervently.

"What a beautiful morning it is!" murmured Robert, feeling that some remark was due from him. "Am I walking too fast for you—Miss Cannon?"

"Oh, no."

He proposed a boat on the river after lunch, and it appeared that Miss Cannon would love it, but Ethel and Mrs. Clive would rather stay on the bank.

His cup of bliss was full. It would be his opportunity of sealing a lifelong friendship with her, or arranging a regular correspondence, and hinting at his ultimate intentions. He must tell her that, of course, while he was at college he was not in a position to offer his heart and hand, but if she could wait. . . . He began to compose speeches in his mind.

They reached the bank and opened the luncheon baskets. Unhampered by Robert, the cook had surpassed herself.

They spread the white cloth and took up their positions around it under the shade of the trees.

Just as Robert was taking up a plate of sandwiches to hand them with a courteous gesture to Miss Cannon, his eyes fell upon the long, white road leading from the village to the riverside and remained fixed there, his face frozen with horror. The hand that held the plate dropped lifelessly back again on to the table-cloth. The eyes of the rest of the party followed his. A curious figure was cycling along the road—a figure with blackened face and a few drooping feathers on its head, and a doormat flying in the wind. A crowd of small children ran behind cheering. It was a figure vaguely familiar to them all.

"It can't be," said Robert hoarsely, passing a hand over his brow.

No one spoke.

It came nearer and nearer. There was no mistaking it. "William!" gasped four voices.

William came to the end of the road. He did not turn aside to either of the roads by the riverside. He did not even recognise or look at them. With set face he rode on to the river bank, and straight amongst them. They fled from before his charge. He rode over the table-cloth, over the sandwiches, patties, rolls and cakes, down the bank and into the river.

They rescued him and the bicycle. Fate was against Robert even there. It was a passing boatman who performed the rescue. William emerged soaked to the skin, utterly exhausted, but feeling vaguely heroic. He was not in the least surprised to see them. He would have been surprised at nothing. Robert wiped and examined his battered bicycle in impotent fury in the background, while Miss Cannon pillowed William's dripping head on her arm, fed him on hot coffee and sandwiches and called him "My poor darling Red Hand!"

She insisted on going home with him. All through the

journey she sustained the character of his faithful squaw. Then, leaving a casual invitation to Robert and Ethel to come over to tea, she departed to pack.

Mrs. Brown descended the stairs from William's room with a tray on which reposed a half-empty bowl of gruel, and met Robert in the hall.

"Robert," she remonstrated, "you really needn't look so upset."

Robert glared at her and laughed a hollow laugh.

"Upset!" he echoed, outraged by the inadequacy of the expression. "You'd be upset if your life was ruined. You'd be upset. I've a *right* to be upset."

He passed his hand desperately through his already ruffled hair.

"You're going there to tea," she reminded him.

"Yes," he said bitterly, "with other people. Who can talk with other people there? No one can. I'd have talked to her on the river. I'd got heaps of things ready in my mind to say. And William comes along and spoils my whole life—and my bicycle. And she's the most beautiful girl I've ever seen in my life. And I've wanted a new bicycle for ever so long and now it's not fit to ride."

"But poor William has caught a very bad chill, dear, so you oughtn't to feel bitter towards him. And he'll have to pay for your bicycle being mended. He'll have no pocket-money till it's paid for."

"You'd think," said Robert with a despairing gesture in the direction of the hall table and apparently addressing it, "you'd think four grown-up people in a house could keep a boy of William's age in order, wouldn't you? You'd think he wouldn't be allowed to go about spoiling people's lives and—and ruining their bicycles. Well, he jolly well won't do it again," he ended darkly.

Mrs. Brown proceeded in the direction of the kitchen.

"Robert," she said soothingly over her shoulder, "you surely want to be at peace with your little brother, when he's not well, don't you?"

"Peace?" he said. Robert turned his haggard countenance upon her as though his ears must have deceived him. "*Peace!* I'll wait. I'll wait till he's all right and going about; I won't start till then. But—peace! It's not peace, it's an *armistice*—that's all."

CHAPTER 3

WILLIAM BELOW STAIRS

WILLIAM was feeling embittered with life in general. He was passing through one of his not infrequent periods of unpopularity. The climax had come with the gift of sixpence bestowed on him by a timid aunt, who hoped thus to purchase his goodwill. With the sixpence he had bought a balloon adorned with the legs and head of a duck fashioned in cardboard. This could be blown up to its fullest extent and then left to subside. It took several minutes to subside, and during those minutes it emitted a long-drawn-out and high-pitched groan. The advantage of this was obvious. William could blow it up to its fullest extent in private and leave it to subside in public concealed beneath his coat. While this was going on, William looked round as though in bewildered astonishment. He inflated it before he went to breakfast. He then held it firmly and secretly so as to keep it inflated till he was sitting at the table. Then he let it subside. His mother knocked over a cup of coffee, and his father cut himself with the bread knife. Ethel, his elder sister, indulged in a mild form of nervous breakdown. William sat with a face of startled innocence. But nothing enraged his family so much as William's expression of innocence. They fell upon him, and he defended himself as well as he could. Yes, he was holding the balloon under the table. Well, he'd blown it up some time ago. He couldn't keep it blown up for ever. He had to let the air out some time. He couldn't help it making a noise when the air went out. It was the way it was made. He hadn't made it. He set off to school with an air of injured innocence—and the balloon. Observing an elderly and irascible-looking gentleman in front of him, he went a few steps down a back street, blew up his balloon, and held it tightly under his coat. Then, when abreast of the old gentleman, he let it off. The old gentleman gave a leap into the air and glared fiercely around. He glanced at the small virtuous-looking schoolboy with obviously no instrument of torture at his lips, and then concentrated his glare of fury and suspicion on the upper windows. William hastened on to the next pedestrian. He had quite a happy walk to school.

School was at first equally successful. William opened his desk, hastily inflated his balloon, closed his desk, then gazed round with his practised expression of horrified astonishment at what followed. He drove the French master to distraction.

"Step out 'oo makes the noise," he screamed.

No one stepped out, and the noise continued at intervals.

The mathematics master finally discovered and confiscated the balloon.

"I hope," said his father at lunch, "that they've taken away that infernal machine of yours."

William replied sadly that they had. He added that some people didn't seem to think it was stealing to take other people's things.

"Then we may look forward to a little peace this evening?" said his father politely. "Not that it matters to me, as I'm going out to dinner. The only thing that relieves the tedium of going out to dinner is the fact that for a short time one has a rest from William."

William acknowledged the compliment by a scowl and a mysterious muttered remark to the effect that some people were always getting at him.

During preparation in afternoon school he read a story-book kindly lent him by his next-door neighbour. It was not because he had no work to do that William read a story-book in preparation. It was a mark of defiance to the world in general. It was also a very interesting story-book. It opened with the hero as a small boy misunderstood and ill-treated by everyone around him. Then he ran away. He went to sea, and in a few years made an immense fortune in the goldfields. He returned in the last chapter and forgave his family and presented them with a noble mansion and several shiploads of gold. The idea impressed William—all except the end part. He thought he'd prefer to have the noble mansion himself and pay rare visits to his family, during which he would listen to their humble apologies, and perhaps give them a nugget or two, but not very much —certainly not much to Ethel. He wasn't sure whether he'd ever really forgive them. He'd have rooms full of squeaky balloons and trumpets in his house anyway, and he'd keep caterpillars and white rats all over the place too— things they made such a fuss about in their old house—and he'd always go about in dirty boots, and he'd never brush his hair or wash, and he'd own dozens of motor cars, and he wouldn't let Ethel go out in any of them. He was roused from this enthralling day-dream by the discovery and confiscation of his story-book by the master in charge, and the subsequent fury of its owner. In order adequately to express his annoyance, he dropped a little ball of blotting-paper soaked in ink down William's back. William, on attempting retaliation, was sentenced to stay in half an hour after school. He returned gloomily to his history book (upside down) and his misanthropic view of life. He compared himself bitterly with the hero of the story-book and decided not to waste another moment of his life in uncongenial surroundings. He made a firm determination to run away as soon as he was released from school.

He walked briskly down the road away from the village. In his pocket reposed the balloon. He had made the cheering discovery that the mathematics master had left it on his desk, so he had joyfully taken it again into his possession. He thought he might reach the coast before night and get

44

to the goldfields before next week. He didn't suppose it took long to make a fortune there. He might be back before next Christmas and—crumbs! he'd jolly well make people sit up. He wouldn't go to school, for one thing, and he'd be jolly careful who he gave nuggets to for another. He'd give nuggets to the butcher's boy and the postman, and the man who came to tune the piano, and the chimney-sweep. He wouldn't give any to any of his family, or any of the masters at the school. He'd just serve people out the way they served him. He just would. The road to the coast seemed long, and he was growing rather tired. He walked in a ditch for a change, and then scraped through a hedge and took a short-cut across a ploughed field. Dusk was falling fast, and even William's buoyant spirits began to flag. The fortune part was all very well, but in the mean-time he was cold and tired and hungry. He hadn't yet reached the coast, much less the goldfields. Something must be done. He remembered that the boy in the story had "begged his way" to the coast. William determined to beg his. But at present there seemed nothing to beg it from, except a hawthorn hedge and a scarecrow in the field behind it. He wandered on disconsolately, deciding to begin his career as a beggar at the first sign of human habitation.

At last he discerned a pair of iron gates through the dusk and, assuming an expression of patient suffering calculated to melt a heart of stone, walked up the drive. At the front door he smoothed down his hair (he had lost his cap on the way), pulled up his stockings, and rang the bell. After an interval a stout gentleman in the garb of a butler opened the door and glared ferociously down at William.

"Please—" began William plaintively.

The stout gentleman interrupted.

"If you're the new Boots," he said majestically, "go round to the back door. If you're not, go away."

He then shut the door in William's face. William, on the top step, considered the question for a few minutes. It was dark and cold, with every prospect of becoming darker and colder. He decided to be the new Boots. He found his way round to the back door and knocked firmly. It was opened by a large woman in a print dress and apron.

"What y' want?" she said aggressively.

"He said," said William firmly, "to come round if I was the new Boots."

The woman surveyed him in grim disapproval.

"You bin round to the front?" she said. "Nerve!"

Her disapproval increased to suspicion.

"Where's your things?" she said.

"Comin'," said William, without a moment's hesitation.

"Too tired to bring 'em with you?" she said sarcastically. "All right. Come in!"

William came in gratefully. It was a large, warm, clean kitchen. A small kitchenmaid was peeling potatoes at a sink, and a housemaid in black, with a frilled cap and apron, was powdering her nose before a glass on the wall. They both turned to stare at William.

" 'Ere's the new Boots," announced Cook. " 'Is valet's bringin' 'is things later."

The housemaid's eye travelled up William from his muddy boots to his untidy hair, then down William from his untidy hair to his muddy boots.

"Imperdent-lookin' child," she commented haughtily, returning to her task.

William decided inwardly that she was to have no share at all in the nuggets.

The kitchenmaid giggled and winked at William, with obviously friendly intent. William mentally promised her half a ship-load of nuggets.

"Now, then, Smutty," said the housemaid without turning round, "none of your sauce!"

" 'Ad your tea?" said the cook to William. William's spirits rose.

"No," he said plaintively.

"All right. Sit down at the table."

William's spirits soared sky-high.

46

He sat at the table and the cook put a large plate of bread and butter before him.

William set to work at once. The housemaid regarded him scornfully.

"Learnt 'is way of eatin' at the zoo," she said pityingly.

The kitchenmaid giggled again and gave William another wink. William had given himself up to whole-hearted epicurean enjoyment of his bread and butter and took no notice of them. At this moment the butler entered.

He subjected the quite unmoved William to another long survey.

"When next you come a-hentering of this 'ouse, my boy," he said, "kindly remember that the front door is reserved for gentry an' the back for brats."

William merely looked at him coldly over a hunk of bread and butter. Mentally he knocked him off the list of nugget-receivers.

The butler looked sadly round the room.

"They're all the same," he lamented. "Eat, eat, eat. Nothin' but eat. Eat all day an' eat all night. 'E's not bin in the 'ouse two minutes an' 'e's at it. Eat! eat eat! 'E'll 'ave all the buttons bust off his uniform in a week like wot the larst one 'ad. Like eatin' better than workin', don't you?" he said sarcastically to William.

"Yes, I do, too," said William with firm conviction.

The kitchenmaid giggled again, and the housemaid gave a sigh expressive of scorn and weariness as she drew a thin pencil over her eyebrows.

"Well, if you've quite finished, my lord," said the butler with ponderous irony, "I'll show you to your room."

William indicated that he had quite finished and was led up to a very small bedroom. Over a chair lay a page's uniform with the conventional row of brass buttons down the front of the coat.

"Togs," explained the butler briefly. "Your togs. Fix 'em on quick as you can. There's company to dinner to-night."

William fixed them on.

"You're smaller than wot the last one was," said the butler critically. "They 'ang a bit loose. Never mind. With a week or two of stuffin' you'll 'ave most probable bust 'em, so it's as well to 'ang loose first. Now, come on. 'Oo's bringing over your things?"

"E—a friend," explained William.

"I suppose it *is* a bit too much to expeck you to carry your own parcels," went on the butler, "in these 'ere days. Bloomin' anarchist, I speck, aren't you?"

William condescended to explain himself.

"I'm a gold-digger," he said.

"Crikey!" said the butler.

William was led down again to the kitchen.

The butler threw open a door that led to a small pantry.

"This 'ere is where you work, and this 'ere," pointing to a large kitchen, "is where you live. You 'ave not," he ended haughtily, "the hentry into the servants' 'all."

"Crumbs!" said William.

"You might as well begin at once," went on the butler; "there's all this lunch's knives to clean. 'Ere's a hapron, 'ere's the knife-board, an' 'ere's the knife-powder."

He shut the bewildered William into the small pantry and turned to the cook.

"What do you think of 'im?" he said.

" 'E looks," said the cook gloomily, "the sort of boy we'll 'ave trouble with."

"Not much clarse," said the housemaid, arranging her frilled apron. "It surprises me 'ow any creature like a boy can grow into an experienced, sensible, broad-minded man like you, Mr. Biggs."

Mr. Biggs simpered and straightened his necktie.

"Well," he admitted, "as a boy, of course, I wasn't like 'im."

Here the pantry door opened and William's face, plentifully adorned with knife-powder, came round.

"I've done some of the knives," he said. "Shall I be doin' something else and finish the others afterwards?"

" 'Ow many 'ave you done?" said Mr. Biggs.

"One or two," said William vaguely, then with a concession to accuracy; "well, two. But I'm feeling tired of doin' knives."

The kitchenmaid emitted a scream of delight and the cook heaved a deep sigh.

The butler advanced slowly and majestically towards William's tousled head, which was still craned around the pantry door.

"You'll finish them knives, my boy," he said, "or—"

William considered the weight and size of Mr. Biggs.

"All right," he said pacifically. "I'll finish the knives."

He disappeared, closing the pantry door behind him.

" 'E's goin' to be a trile," said the cook, "an' no mistake."

"Trile's 'ardly the word," said Mr. Biggs.

"Haffliction," supplied the housemaid.

"That's more like it," said Mr. Biggs.

Here William's head appeared again.

"Wot time's supper?" he said.

He retired precipitately at a hysterical shriek from the kitchenmaid and a roar of fury from the butler.

"You'd better go an' do your potatoes in the pantry," said the cook to the kitchenmaid, "and let's 'ave a bit of peace in 'ere; and see 'e's doin' of 'is work all right."

The kitchenmaid departed joyfully to the pantry.

William was sitting by the table, idly toying with a knife. He had experimented upon the knife-powder by mixing it with water, and the little brown pies that were the result lay in a row on the mantelpiece. He had also tasted it, as the dark stains upon his lips testified. His hair was standing straight up on his head as it always did when life was strenuous. He began the conversation.

"You'd be surprised," he said, "if you knew what I really was."

She giggled.

"Go on!" she said. "What are you?"

"I'm a gold-digger," he said. "I've got ship-loads an'

ship-loads of gold. At least, I will have soon. I'm not goin'
to give *him*," pointing towards the door, "any, nor any of
them in there."

"Wot about me?" said the kitchenmaid, winking at the
cat as the only third person to be let into the joke.

"You," said William graciously, "shall have a whole lot
of nuggets. Look here." With a princely flourish he took
up a knife and cut off three buttons from the middle of his
coat and gave them to her. "You keep those and they'll be
kind of tokens. See? When I come home rich you show me
the buttons an' I'll remember and give you the nuggets.
See? I'll maybe marry you," he promised, "if I've not
married anyone else."

The kitchenmaid put her head round the pantry door.
" 'E's loony," she said. "But it's lovely listening to
'im talkin'."

Further conversation was prevented by the ringing of the
front door bell and the arrival of the "company."

Mr. Biggs and the housemaid departed to do the honours.
The kitchenmaid ran to help with the dishing up, and
William was left sitting on the pantry table, idly making
patterns in knife-powder with his finger.

"Wot was 'e doin'?" said the cook to the kitchenmaid.

"Nothin'—'cept talkin'," said the kitchenmaid. " 'E's a
tonic, *'e* is," she added.

"If you've finished the knives," called out the cook,
"there's some boots and shoes on the floor to be done.
Brushes an' blacking on the shelf."

William arose with alacrity. He thought boots would be
more interesting than knives. He carefully concealed the
pile of uncleaned knives behind the knife-box and began
on the shoes.

The butler returned.

"Soup ready?" he said. "The company's just goin' into
the dining-room—a pal of the master's. Decent-lookin'
bloke," he added patronisingly.

William, in his pantry, had covered a brush very thickly

with blacking and was putting it in heavy layers on the boots and shoes. A large part of it adhered to his own hands. The butler looked in at him.

"Wot's 'appened to your buttons?" he said sternly.

"Come off," said William.

"Bust off," corrected the butler. "I said so soon as I saw you. I said you'd 'ave eat your buttons bust off in a week. Well, you've eat 'em bust off in ten minutes."

"Eatin' an' destroyin' of 'is clothes," he said gloomily, returning to the kitchen. "It's all boys ever do—eatin' an' destroyin' of their clothes."

He went out with the soup and William was left with the boots. He was getting tired of boots. He'd covered them all thickly with blacking, and he didn't know what to do next. Then suddenly he remembered his balloon in his pocket upstairs. It might serve to vary the monotony of life. He slipped quietly upstairs for it, and then returned to his boots.

Soon Mr. Biggs and the housemaid returned with the empty soup-plates. Then through the kitchen resounded a high-pitched squeal, dying away slowly and shrilly.

The housemaid screamed.

"Lawks!" said the cook, "someone's atorchurin' of the poor cat to death. It'll be that blessed boy."

The butler advanced manfully and opened the pantry door. William stood holding in one hand an inflated balloon with the cardboard head and legs of a duck.

The butler approached him.

"If you let off that there thing once more, you little varmint," he said, "I'll—"

Threateningly he had advanced his large expanse of countenance very close to William's. Acting upon a sudden uncontrollable impulse, William took up the brush thickly smeared with blacking and pushed back Mr. Biggs's face with it.

There was a moment's silence of sheer horror, then Mr. Biggs hurled himself furiously upon William . . .

In the dining-room sat the master and mistress of the house and their guest.

"Did the new Boots arrive?" said the master to his wife.

"Yes," she said.

"Any good?" he said.

"He doesn't seem to have impressed Biggs very favourably," she said, "but they never do."

"The human boy," said the guest, "is given us as a discipline. I possess one. Though he is my own son, I find it difficult to describe the atmosphere of peace and relief that pervades the house when he is out of it."

"I'd like to meet your son," said the host.

"You probably will, sooner or later," said the guest gloomily. "Everyone in the neighbourhood meets him sooner or later. He does not hide his light under a bushel. Personally, I prefer people who haven't met him. They can't judge me by him."

At this moment the butler came in with a note.

"No answer," he said, and departed with his slow dignity.

"Excuse me," said the lady as she opened it, "it's from my sister. 'I hope,' she read, 'that you aren't inconvenienced much by the non-arrival of the Boots I engaged for you. He's got 'flu.' But he's come," she said wonderingly.

There came the sound of an angry shout, a distant scream and the clattering of heavy running footsteps . . . coming nearer . . .

Presently the door was burst open and in rushed a boy with a blacking brush in one hand and an inflated balloon in the other. He was much dishevelled, with three buttons off the front of his uniform, and his face streaked with knife-powder and blacking. Behind him ran a fat butler, his face purple with fury beneath a large smear of blacking. The boy rushed round the table, slipped on the polished floor, clutched desperately at the neck of the guest, bringing both guest and chair down upon the floor beside him. In a sudden silence of utter paralysed horror, guest and boy sat on the floor and stared at each other. Then the boy's nerveless hand relaxed its hold upon the balloon, which had somehow or other survived the vicissitudes of the flight, and a shrill squeak rang through the silence of the room.

The master and mistress of the house sat looking round in dazed astonishment.

As the guest looked at the boy there appeared on his countenance amazement, then incredulity, and finally frozen horror. As the boy looked at the guest there appeared on his countenance amazement, then incredulity, and finally blank dejection.

"Good Lord!" said the guest, "it's *William*!"

"Oh, crumbs!" said the Boots, "it's *Father*!"

CHAPTER 4

THE FALL OF THE IDOL

WILLIAM was bored. He sat at his desk in the sunny schoolroom and gazed dispassionately at a row of figures on the blackboard.

"It isn't *sense*," he murmured scornfully.

Miss Drew was also bored, but, unlike William, she tried to hide the fact.

"If the interest on a hundred pounds for one year is five pounds," she said wearily, then, "William Brown, do sit up and don't look so stupid!"

William changed his position from that of lolling over one side of his desk to that of lolling over the other, and began to justify himself.

"Well, I can't unner*stand* any of it. It's enough to make anyone look stupid when he can't unner*stand* any of it. I can't think why people go on givin' people bits of money for givin' 'em lots of money and go on an' on doin' it. It dun't seem sense. Anyone's a mug for givin' anyone a hundred pounds just 'cause he says he'll go on givin' him five pounds and go on stickin' to his hundred pounds. How's he to *know* he will? Well," he warmed to his subject, "what's to stop him not givin' any five pounds once he's got hold of the hundred pounds an' goin' on stickin' to the hundred pounds—"

Miss Drew checked him by a slim, upraised hand.

"William," she said patiently, "just listen to me. Now suppose," her eyes roved round the room and settled on a small red-haired boy, "suppose that Eric wanted a hundred pounds for something and you lent it to him—"

"I wun't lend Eric a hundred pounds," he said firmly, " 'cause I ha'n't got it. I've only got 3½d, an' I wun't lend that to Eric, 'cause I'm not such a mug, 'cause I lent him my mouth-organ once an' he bit a bit off an'—"

Miss Drew interrupted sharply. Teaching on a hot afternoon is rather trying.

"You'd better stay in after school, William, and I'll explain."

William scowled, emitted his monosyllable of scornful disdain, "Huh!" and relapsed into gloom.

He brightened, however, on remembering a lizard he had caught on the way to school, and drew it from its hiding-place in his pocket. But the lizard had abandoned the unequal struggle for existence among the stones, top, penknife, bits of putty, and other small objects that inhabited William's pocket. The housing problem had been too much for it.

William, in disgust, shrouded the remains in blotting-paper and disposed of it in his neighbour's ink-pot. The neighbour protested and an enlivening scrimmage ensued.

Finally the lizard was dropped down the neck of an inveterate enemy of William's in the next row, and was extracted only with the help of obliging friends. Threats of vengeance followed, couched in blood-curdling terms and written on blotting-paper.

Meanwhile Miss Drew explained Simple Interest to a small but earnest coterie of admirers in the front row. And William, in the back row, whiled away the hours.

But his turn was to come.

At the end of afternoon school one by one the class departed, leaving William only, nonchalantly chewing an india-rubber and glaring at Miss Drew.

"Now, William."

Miss Drew was severely patient.

William went up and stood by her desk.

"You see, if someone borrows a hundred pounds from someone else—"

She wrote down the figures on a piece of paper, bending low over her desk. The sun poured in through the window, showing the little golden curls on the nape of her neck. She lifted to William eyes that were stern and frowning, but blue as blue above flushed cheeks.

"Don't you *see*, William?" she said.

There was a faint perfume about her, and William the devil-may-care pirate and robber-chief, the stern despiser of all things effeminate, felt the first dart of the malicious, blind god. He blushed and simpered.

"Yes, I see all about it now," he assured her. "You've explained it all plain now. I cudn't unner*stand* it before. It's a bit soft—in't it—anyway, to go lending hundred pounds about just 'cause someone says they'll give you five pounds next year. Some folks is mugs. But I do unner*stand* now. I cudn't unnerstand it before."

"You'd have found it simpler if you hadn't played with dead lizards all the time," she said wearily, closing her books.

William gasped.

He went home her devoted slave. Certain members of the class always deposited dainty bouquets on her desk in the morning. William was determined to outshine the rest. He went into the garden with a large basket and a pair of scissors the next morning before he set out for school.

It happened that no one was about. He went first to the hothouse. It was a riot of colour. He worked there with a thoroughness and concentration worthy of a nobler cause. He came out staggering beneath a piled-up basket of hothouse blooms. The hothouse itself was bare and desolate.

Hearing a sound in the back garden, he hastily decided to delay no longer, but to set out to school at once. He set out as unostentatiously as possible.

Miss Drew, entering her classroom, was aghast to see instead of the usual small array of buttonholes on her desk, a mass of already withering hothouse flowers completely covering her desk and chair.

William was a boy who never did things by halves.

"Good Heavens!" she cried in consternation.

William blushed with pleasure.

He changed his seat to one in the front row. All that morning he sat, his eyes fixed on her earnestly, dreaming of moments in which he rescued her from robbers and pirates (here he was somewhat inconsistent with his own favourite *rôle* of robber-chief and pirate), and bore her fainting in his strong arms to safety. Then she clung to him in love and gratitude, and they were married at once by the Archbishops of Canterbury and York.

William would have no half-measures. They were to be married by the Archbishops of Canterbury and York, or else the Pope. He wasn't sure that he wouldn't rather have the Pope. He would wear his black pirate suit with the skull-and-crossbones. No, that would not do—

"What have I just been saying, William?" said Miss Drew.

William coughed and gazed at her soulfully.

" 'Bout lendin' money?" he said hopefully.

"William!" she snapped. "This isn't an arithmetic lesson. I'm trying to teach you about the Armada."

"Oh, *that*!" said William brightly and ingratiatingly. "Oh, yes."

"Tell me something about it."

"I don't *know* anything—not jus' yet—"

"I've been *telling* you about it. I do wish you'd listen," she said despairingly.

William relapsed into silence, nonplussed, but by no means cowed.

When he reached home that evening he found that the garden was the scene of excitement and hubbub. One policeman was measuring the panes of glass in the conservatory door, and another was on his knees examining the beds near. His elder sister, Ethel, was standing at the front door.

"Every single flower has been stolen from the conservatory some time this morning," she said excitedly. "We've only just been able to get the police. William, did you see anyone about when you went to school this morning?"

William pondered deeply. His most guileless and innocent expression came to his face.

"No," he said at last. "No, Ethel, I didn't see nobody." William coughed and discreetly withdrew.

That evening he settled down at the table, spreading out his books around him, a determined frown upon his small face.

His father was sitting in an arm-chair by the window reading the evening paper.

"Father," said William suddenly, "s'pose I came to you an' said you was to give me a hundred pounds an' I'd give you five pounds next year an' so on, would you give it me?"

"I should not, my son," said his father firmly.

William sighed.

"I knew there was something wrong with it," he said. Mr. Brown returned to the leading article, but not for long.

"Father, what was the date of the Armada?"

"Good Heavens! How should I know? I wasn't there." William sighed.

"Well, I'm tryin' to write about it and why it failed an'— why did it fail?"

Mr. Brown groaned, gathered up his paper, and retired to the dining-room.

He had almost finished the leading article when William appeared, his arms full of books, and sat down quietly at the table.

"Father, what's the French for 'my aunt is walking in the garden'?"

"What on earth are you doing?" said Mr. Brown irritably.

"I'm doing my home-work." said William virtuously.

"I never even knew you got any to do."

"No," William admitted gently, "I don't generally

58

bother much about it, but I'm goin' to now—'cause Miss Drew"—he blushed slightly and paused—" 'cause Miss Drew"—he blushed more deeply and began to stammer—" 'c—'cause Miss Drew"—he was almost apoplectic.

Mr. Brown gathered quietly up his paper and crept out to the veranda, where his wife sat with the week's mending.

"William's gone raving mad in the dining-room," he said pleasantly, as he sat down. "Takes the form of a wild thirst for knowledge, and a babbling of a Miss Drawing, or Drew, or something. He's best left alone."

Mrs. Brown merely smiled placidly over the mending.

Mr. Brown had finished one leading article and begun another before William appeared again. He stood in the doorway frowning and stern.

"Father, what's the capital of Holland?"

"Good Heavens!" said his father. "Buy him an encyclopedia. Anything, anything. What does he think I am? What—"

"I'd better set apart a special room for his homework," said Mrs. Brown soothingly, "now that he's beginning to take such an interest."

"A room!" echoed his father bitterly. "He wants a whole house."

Miss Drew was surprised, and touched, by William's earnestness and attention the next day. At the end of the afternoon school he kindly offered to carry her books home for her. He waved aside all protests. He marched home by her side discoursing pleasantly, his small, freckled face beaming devotion.

"I like pirates, don't you, Miss Drew? An' robbers an' things like that? Miss Drew, would you like to be married to a robber?"

He was trying to reconcile his old, beloved dream of his future estate with the new one of becoming Miss Drew's husband.

"No," she said firmly.

His heart sank.

"Nor a pirate?" he said sadly.

"No."

"They're quite nice really—pirates," he assured her.

"I think not."

"Well," he said resignedly, "we'll jus' have to go huntin' wild animals and things. That'll be all right."

"Who?" she said, bewildered.

"Well—jus' you wait," he said darkly.

Then: "Would you rather be married by the Archbishop of York or the Pope?"

"The Archbishop, I think," she said gravely.

He nodded.

"All right."

She was distinctly amused. She was less amused the next evening. Miss Drew had a male cousin—a very nice-looking male cousin, with whom she often went for walks in the evening. This evening, by chance, they passed William's house, and William, who was in the garden, threw aside his temporary *rôle* of pirate and joined them. He trotted happily on the other side of Miss Drew. He entirely monopolised the conversation. The male cousin seemed to encourage him, and this annoyed Miss Drew. He refused to depart in spite of Miss Drew's strong hints. He had various items of interest to impart, and he imparted them with the air of one assured of an appreciative hearing. He had found a dead rat the day before and given it to his dog, but his dog didn't like 'em dead and neither did the ole cat, so he'd buried it. Did Miss Drew like all those flowers he'd got her the other day? He was afraid that he cudn't bring any more like that jus' yet. Were there pirates now? Well, what would folks do to one if there was one? He didn't see why there shun't be pirates now. He thought he'd start it, anyway. He'd like to shoot a lion. He was goin' to one day. He'd shoot a lion an' a tiger. He'd bring the skin home to Miss Drew, if she liked. He grew recklessly generous. He'd bring home lots of skins of all sorts of animals for Miss Drew.

"Don't you think you ought to be going home, William?"

said Miss Drew coldly.

William hastened to reassure her.

"Oh, no—not for ever so long yet," he said.

"Isn't it your bedtime?"

"Oh, no—not yet—not for ever so long."

The male cousin was giving William his whole attention.

"What does Miss Drew teach you at school, William?" he said.

"Oh, jus' ornery things. Armadas an' things. An' 'bout lending a hundred pounds. That's a norful *soft* thing. I unner*stand* it," he added hastily, fearing further explanation, "but it's *soft*. My father thinks it is too, an' he oughter *know*. He's bin abroad lots of times. He's bin chased by a bull, my father has—"

The shades of night were falling fast when William reached Miss Drew's house, still discoursing volubly. He was drunk with success. He interpreted his idol's silence as the silence of rapt admiration.

He was passing through the gate with his two companions with the air of one assured of welcome, when Miss Drew shut the gate upon him firmly.

"You'd better go home now, William," she said.

William hesitated.

"I don't mind comin' in a bit," he said. "I'm not tired."

But Miss Drew and the male cousin were already halfway up the walk.

William turned his steps homeward. He met Ethel near the gate.

"William, where *have* you been? I've been looking for you everywhere. It's *hours* past your bedtime."

"I was goin' a walk with Miss Drew."

"But you should have come home at your bedtime."

"I don't think she wanted me to go," he said with dignity. "I think it wun't of bin p'lite."

William found that a new and serious element had entered his life. It was not without its disadvantages. Many had been the little diversions by which William had been wont to while away the hours of instruction. In spite of his devotion to Miss Drew, he missed the old days of carefree exuberance, but he kept his new seat in the front row and clung to his *rôle* of earnest student. He was beginning to find, also, that a conscientious performance of home-lessons limited his activities after school hours, but at present he hugged his chains. Miss Drew, from her seat on the platform, found William's soulful concentrated gaze somewhat embarrassing, and his questions even more so.

As he went out of school he heard her talking to another mistress.

"I'm very fond of syringa," she was saying. "I'd love to have some."

William decided to bring her syringa, handfuls of syringa, armfuls of syringa.

He went straight home to the gardener.

"No, I ain't got no syringa. Please step off my rose-bed, Mister William. No, there ain't any syringa in this 'ere garding. I dunno for why. Please leave my 'ose pipe alone, Mister William."

"Huh!" ejaculated William, scornfully turning away.

He went round the garden. The gardener had been quite right. There were guelder roses everywhere, but no syringa.

He climbed the fence and surveyed the next garden. There were guelder roses everywhere, but no syringa. It must have been some peculiarity in the soil.

William strolled down the road, scanning the gardens as he went. All had guelder roses. None had syringa.

Suddenly he stopped.

On the table in the window of a small house at the bottom of the road was a vase of syringa. He did not know who lived there. He entered the garden cautiously. No one was about.

He looked into the room. It was empty. The window was open at the bottom.

He scrambled in, removing several layers of white paint from the window-sill as he did so. He was determined to have that syringa. He took it dripping from the vase, and was preparing to depart when the door opened and a fat woman appeared upon the threshold. The scream that she emitted at sight of William curdled the very blood in his veins. She dashed to the window, and William, in self-defence, dodged round the table and out of the door. The back door was open and William blindly fled by it. The fat woman did not pursue. She was leaning out of the window, and her shrieks rent the air.

"Police! Help! Murder! Robbers!"

The quiet little street rang with the raucous sounds.

William felt cold shivers creeping up and down his pine. He was in a small back garden from which he could see no exit.

Meanwhile the shrieks were redoubled.

"Help! *Help! Help!*"

Then came sounds of the front door opening and men's voices.

"Hello! Who is it? What is it?"

William glared round wildly. There was a hen-house in the corner of the garden, and into this he dashed, tearing open the door and plunging through a mass of flying feathers and angry, disturbed hens.

William crouched in a corner of the dark hen-house determinedly clutching his bunch of syringa.

Distant voices were at first all he could hear. Then they came nearer, and he heard the fat lady's voice loudly declaiming.

"He was quite a small man, but with such an evil face. I just had one glimpse of him as he dashed past me. I'm sure he'd have murdered me if I hadn't cried for help. Oh, the coward! And a poor, defenceless woman! He was standing by the silver table. I disturbed him at his work of crime. I feel so upset. I shan't sleep for nights. I shall see his evil, murderous face. And a poor, unarmed woman!"

"Can you give us no details, madam?" said a man's voice. "Could you recognise him again?"

"Anywhere!" she said firmly. "Such a criminal face. You've no idea how upset I am. I might have been a lifeless corpse now, if I hadn't had the courage to cry for help."

"We're measuring the footprints, madam. You say he went out by the front door?"

"I'm convinced he did. I'm convinced he's hiding in the bushes by the gate. Such a low face. My nerves are absolutely jarred."

"We'll search the bushes again, madam," said the other voice wearily, "but I expect he has escaped by now."

"The brute!" said the fat lady. "Oh, the *brute*! And that *face*. If I hadn't had the courage to cry out—"

The voices died away and William was left alone in a corner of the hen-house.

A white hen appeared in the little doorway, squawked at him angrily, and retired, cackling indignation. Visions of life-long penal servitude or hanging passed before William's eyes. He'd rather be executed, really. He hoped they'd execute him.

Then he heard the fat lady bidding good-bye to the policeman. Then she came to the back garden evidently with a friend, and continued to pour forth her troubles.

"And he *dashed* past me, dear. Quite a small man, but with such an evil face."

A black hen appeared in the little doorway, and with an angry squawk at William, returned to the back garden.

"I think you're *splendid*, dear," said the invisible friend. "How you had the *courage*! . . ."

The white hen gave a sardonic scream.

"You'd better come in and rest, darling," said the friend.

"I'd better," said the fat lady in a plaintive, suffering voice. "I do feel very . . . shaken . . ."

Their voices ceased, the door was closed, and all was still.

Cautiously, very cautiously, a much-dishevelled William crept from the hen-house and round the side of the house. Here he found a locked side-gate over which he climbed, and very quietly he glided down to the front gate and to the road.

"Where's William this evening?" said Mrs. Brown. "I do hope he won't stay out after his bedtime."

"Oh, I've just met him," said Ethel. "He was going up to his bedroom. He was covered with hen feathers and holding a bunch of syringa."

"Mad!" sighed his father. "Mad! mad! mad!"

The next morning William laid a bunch of syringa upon Miss Drew's desk. He performed the offering with an air of quiet, manly pride. Miss Drew recoiled.

"*Not* syringa, William. I simply can't *bear* the smell!"

William gazed at her in silent astonishment for a few moments.

Then: "But you *said* . . . you *said* . . . you said you were fond of syringa an' that you'd like to have them."

"Did I say syringa?" said Miss Drew vaguely. "I meant guelder roses."

William's gaze was one of stony contempt.

He went slowly back to his old seat at the back of the room.

That evening he made a bonfire with several choice friends, and played Red Indians in the garden. There was a certain thrill in returning to the old life.

"Hello!" said his father, encountering William creeping on all fours among the bushes. "I thought you did home-work now?"

William arose to an upright position.

"I'm not goin' to bother much about it now," said William. "Miss Drew, she can't talk straight. She dunno what she *means*."

"That's always the trouble with women," agreed his father. "William says his idol has feet of clay," he said to his wife, who had approached.

"I dunno as she's got feet of clay," said William, the literal. "All I say is she can't talk straight. I took no end of trouble an' she dunno what she means. I think her feet's

65

all right. She walks all right. 'Sides, when they make folks false feet, they make 'em of wood, not clay.''

CHAPTER 5

THE SHOW

THE Outlaws sat around the old barn, plunged in deep thought. Henry, the oldest member (aged 12¼) had said in a moment of inspiration:

"Let's think of—sumthin' else to do—sumthin' quite fresh from what we've ever done before."

And the Outlaws were thinking.

They had engaged in mortal combat with one another, they had cooked strange ingredients over a smoking and reluctant flame with a fine disregard for culinary conventions, they had tracked each other over the countryside with gait and complexions intended to represent those of the aborigines of South America, they had even turned their attention to kidnapping (without any striking success), and these occupations had palled.

In all its activities the Society of Outlaws (comprising four members) aimed at a simple, unostentatious mode of procedure. In their shrinking from the glare of publicity they showed an example of unaffected modesty that many other public societies might profitably emulate. The parents of the members were unaware of the very existence of the society. The ill-timed and tactless interference of parents had nipped in the bud many a cherished plan, and by bitter experience the Outlaws had learnt that secrecy was their only protection. Owing to the rules and restrictions of an unsympathetic world that orders school hours from 9 to 4, their meetings were confined to half-holidays and occasionally Sunday afternoons.

William, the ever-ingenious, made the first suggestion.

"Let's shoot things with bows an' arrows same as real outlaws used to," he said.

"What things?" and

"What bows an' arrows?" said Henry and Ginger simultaneously.

"Oh, anything—birds an' cats an' hens an' things—an' buy bows an' arrows. You can buy them in shops."

"We can make them," said Douglas hopefully.

"Not like you can get them in shops. They'd shoot crooked or sumthin' if we made them. They've got to be jus' so to shoot straight. I saw some in Brook's window, too, jus' right—jus' same as real outlaws had."

"How much?" said the Outlaws breathlessly.

"Five shillings—targets for learnin' on before we begin shootin' real things an' all."

"Five shillings!" breathed Douglas. He might as well have said five pounds. "We've not got five shillings. Henry's not having any money since he broke their drawing-room window an' Ginger only has 3d a week an' has to give collection an' we've not paid for the guinea-pig yet, the one that got into Ginger's sister's hat an' she was so mad at, an'—"

"Oh, never mind all that," said William, scornfully. "We'll jus' get five shillings."

"How?"

"Well," uncertainly, "grown-ups can always get money when they want it."

"How?" again.

William disliked being tied down to details.

"Oh—bazaars an' things," impatiently.

"Bazaars!" exploded Henry. "Who'd come to a bazaar if we had one? Who would? Jus' tell me that if you're so clever! Who'd come to it? Besides, you've got to sell things at a bazaar, haven't you? What'd we sell? We've got nothin' to sell, have we? What's the good of havin' a bazaar with nothin' to sell and no one to buy it? Jus' tell me that!"

Henry always enjoyed scoring off William.

"Well—shows an' things," said William desperately.

There was a moment's silence, then Ginger repeated thoughtfully: "Shows!"

"We *could* do a show," he said. "Get animals an' things an' charge money for lookin' at them."

"Who'd pay it?" said Henry, the doubter.

"Anyone would. You'd pay to see animals, wouldn't you?—real animals. People do at the Zoo, don't they? Well, we'll get some animals. That's easy enough, isn't it?"

A neighbouring church clock struck four and the meeting was adjourned.

"Well, we'll have a show an' get money and buy bows an' arrows an' shoot things," summed up William, "an' we'll arrange the show next week."

William returned home slowly and thoughtfully. He sat on his bed, his hands in his pockets, his brow drawn into a frown, his thoughts wandering in a dreamland of wonderful "shows" and rare, exotic beasts.

Suddenly from the next room came a thin sound that gathered volume till it seemed to fill the house like the roaring of a lion, then died gradually away and was followed by silence. But only for a second. It began again— a small whisper that grew louder and louder, became a raucous bellow, then faded slowly away to rise again after a moment's silence. In the next room William's mother's Aunt Emily was taking her afternoon nap. Aunt Emily had come down a month ago for a week's visit and had not yet referred to the date of her departure. William's father was growing anxious. She was a stout, healthy lady, who spent all her time recovering from a slight illness she had had two years ago. Her life held two occupations, and only two. These were eating and sleeping. For William she possessed a subtle but irresistible fascination. Her stature, her appetite, her gloom, added to the fact that she utterly ignored him, attracted him strongly.

The tea-bell rang and the sound of the snoring ceased

abruptly. This entertainment over, William descended to the dining-room, where his father was addressing his mother with some heat.

"Is she going to stay here for ever or only for a few years? I'd like to know, because—"

Perceiving William, he stopped abruptly, and William's mother murmured:

"It's so nice to have her, dear."

Then Aunt Emily entered.

"Have you slept well, Aunt?"

"Slept!" repeated Aunt Emily majestically. "I hardly expect to sleep in my state of health. A little rest is all I can expect."

"Sorry you're no better," said William's father sardonically.

"*Better?*" she repeated again indignantly. "It will be a long time before I'm better."

She lowered her large, healthy frame into a chair, carefully selected a substantial piece of bread and butter and attacked it with vigour.

"I'm going to the post office after tea," said William's mother. "Would you care to come with me?"

Aunt Emily took a large helping of jam.

"You hardly expect me to go out in the evening in my state of health, surely? It's years since I went out after tea. And I was at the post office this morning. There were a lot of people there, but they served me first. I suppose they saw I looked ill."

William's father choked suddenly and apologised, but not humbly.

"Though I must say," went on Aunt Emily, "this place does suit me. I think after a few months here I should be a little stronger. Pass the jam, William."

The glance that William's father fixed upon her would have made a stronger woman quail, but Aunt Emily was scraping out the last remnants of jam and did not notice.

"I'm a bit over-tired to-day, I think," she went on. "I'm

so apt to forget how weak I am and then I overdo it. I'm ready for the cake, William. I just sat out in the sun yesterday afternoon and sat a bit too long and over-tired myself. I ought to write letters after tea, but I don't think I have the strength. Another piece of cake, William. I'll go upstairs to rest instead, I think. I hope you'll keep the house quiet. It's so rarely that I can get a bit of sleep."

William's father left the room abruptly. William sat on and watched, with fascinated eyes, the cake disappear, and finally followed the large, portly figure upstairs and sat down in his room to plan the "show" and incidentally listen, with a certain thrilled awe, for the sounds from next door.

The place and time of the "show" presented no little difficulty. To hold it in the old barn would give away to the world the cherished secret of their meeting-place. It was William who suggested his bedroom, to be entered, not by way of the front door and staircase, but by the less public way of the garden wall and scullery roof. Ever an optimist, he affirmed that no one would see or hear. The choice of a time was limited to Wednesday afternoon, Saturday afternoon, and Sunday. Sunday at first was ruled out as impossible. But there were difficulties about Wednesday afternoon and Saturday afternoon. On Wednesday afternoon Ginger and Douglas were unwilling and ungraceful pupils at a dancing class. On Saturday afternoon William's father gardened and would command a view of the garden wall and scullery roof. On these afternoons also Cook and Emma, both of a suspicious turn of mind, would be at large. On Sunday Cook and Emma went out, William's mother paid a regular weekly visit to an old friend, and William's father spent the afternoon on the sofa, dead to the world.

Moreover, as he pointed out to the Outlaws, the members of the Sunday School could be waylaid and induced to attend the show and they would probably be provided with money for collection. The more William thought over it, the more attractive became the idea of a Sunday afternoon in spite of superficial difficulties; therefore Sunday afternoon was finally chosen.

The day was fortunately a fine one, and William and the other Outlaws were at work early. William had asked his mother, with an expression of meekness and virtue that ought to have warned her of danger, if he might have "jus' a few friends" in his room for the afternoon. His mother, glad that her husband should be spared his son's restless company, gave willing permission.

By half-past two the exhibits were ready. In a cage by the window sat a white rat painted in faint alternate stripes of blue and pink. This was Douglas's contribution, hand-painted by himself in water colours. It wore a bewildered expression and occasionally licked its stripes and then obviously wished it hadn't. Its cage bore a notice printed on cardboard:

> RAT FROM CHINA
> RATS ARE ALL LIKE
> THIS IN CHINA

Next came a cat belonging to William's sister, Smuts by name, now imprisoned beneath a basket-chair. At the best of times Smuts was short-tempered, and all its life had cherished a bitter hatred of William. Now, enclosed by its enemy in a prison two feet square, its fury knew no bounds. It tore at the basket work, it flew wildly round and round, scratching, spitting, swearing. Its chair bore the simple and appropriate notice:

> WILD CAT

William watched it with honest pride and prayed fervently that its indignation would not abate during the afternoon.

Next came a giant composed of Douglas upon Ginger's back, draped in two sheets tied tightly round Douglas's neck. This was labelled:

```
GENWIN·GIANT
```

Ginger was already growing restive. His muffled voice was heard from the folds of the sheets informing the other Outlaws that it was a bit thick and he hadn't known it would be like this or he wouldn't have done it and anyway he was going to change with Douglas half-time or he'd chuck up the whole thing.

The next exhibit was a black fox fur of William's mother's, to which was fortunately attached a head and several feet, and which he had surreptitiously removed from her wardrobe. This had been tied up, stuffed with waste-paper and wired by William till it was, in his eyes, remarkably lifelike. As the legs, even with the assistance of wire, refused to support the body, and the head would only droop sadly to the ground, it was perforce exhibited in a recumbent attitude. It bore marks of sticky fingers, and of several side slips of the scissors when William was cutting the wire, but on the whole he was justly proud of it. It bore the striking but untruthful legend:

```
BEAR SHOT
BY OUTLAWS
·IN RUSHER
```

Next came:

```
BLUE DOG
```

This was Henry's fox terrier, generally known as Chips. For Chips the world was very black. Henry's master-mind had scorned his paint-box and his water colours. Henry had "borrowed" a blue bag and dabbed it liberally over Chips. Chips had, after the first wild, frenzied struggle, offered no resistance. He now sat, a picture of black despair, turning every now and then a melancholy eye upon the still enraged Smuts. But for him cats and joy and life and fighting were no more. He was abject, shamed—a blue dog.

William himself, as showman, was an imposing figure. He was robed in a red dressing-gown of his father's that trailed on the ground behind him and over whose cords in front he stumbled ungracefully as he walked. He had cut a few strands from the fringe of a rug and glued them to his lips to represent moustaches. They fell in two straight lines over his mouth. On his head was a tinsel crown, once worn by his sister as Fairy Queen.

The show had been widely advertised and all the neighbouring children had been individually canvassed, but under strict orders of secrecy. The threats of what the Outlaws would do if their secret were disclosed had kept many a child awake at night.

William surveyed the room proudly.

"Not a bad show for a penny, I *should* say. I guess there aren't many like it, anyway. Do shut up talkin', Ginger. It'll spoil it all, if folks hear the giant talking out of his stomach. It's Douglas that's got to do the giant's *talking*. Anyone could see that. I say, they're comin'! Look! They're comin'! Along the wall!"

There was a thin line of children climbing along the wall in single file on all fours. They ascended the scullery roof and approached the window. These were the first arrivals who had called on their way to Sunday School.

Henry took their pennies and William cleared his throat and began:

"White rat from China, ladies an' gentlemen, pink an' blue striped. All rats is pink an' blue striped in China. This is the only genwin China rat in England—brought over from China special las' week jus' for the show. It lives on

74

China bread an' butter brought over special too."

"Wash it!" jeered an unbeliever. "Jus' wash it an' let's see it then."

"Wash it?" repeated the showman indignantly. "It's gotter be washed. It's washed every morning an' night same as you or me. China rats have gotter be washed or they'd die right off. Washin' 'em don't make no difference to their stripes. Anyone knows that that knows anything about China rats, I guess."

He laughed scornfully and turned to Smuts. Smuts had grown used to the basket-chair and was settling down for a nap. William crouched down on all fours, ran his fingers along the basket-work, and, putting his face close to it, gave vent to a malicious howl. Smuts sprang at him, scratching and spitting.

"Wild cat," said William triumphantly. "Look at it! Kill anyone if it got out! Spring at their throats, it would, an' scratch their eyes out with its paws an' bite their necks till its teeth met. If I jus' moved away that chair it would spring out at you." They moved hastily away from the chair. "And I bet some of you would be dead pretty quick. It could have anyone's head right off with bitin' and scratchin'. Right off—separate from their bodies!"

There was an awe-stricken silence. Then:

"Garn! It's Smuts. It's your sister's cat!"

William laughed as though vastly amused by this idea.

"Smuts!" he said, giving a surreptitious kick to the chair that infuriated its occupant still more. "I guess there wouldn't be many of us left in this house if Smuts was like this."

They passed on to the giant.

"A giant," said William, re-arranging the tinsel crown, which was slightly too big for him. "Real giant. Look at it. As big as two of you put together. How d'you think he gets in at doors and things? Has to have everything made special. Look at him walk. Then in a whisper, "Walk, Ginger!"

Ginger took two steps forward. Douglas clutched his shoulders anxiously.

"Go on," urged William scornfully. "That's not walkin'."

The goaded Ginger's voice came from the giant's middle regions!

"If you go on talkin' at me, I'll drop him. I'm just about sick of it."

"All right," said William hastily.

"Anyway, it's a giant," he went on to his audience. "A jolly fine giant."

"It's got Douglas's face," said one of his audience.

William was for a moment at a loss.

"Well," William said at last, "a giant's got to have some sort of a face, hasn't it? Can't not have a face, can it?"

The Russian Bear, which had often been seen adorning the shoulders of William's mother and was promptly recognised, was greeted with ribald jeers, but there was no doubt as to the success of the Blue Dog. Chips advanced deprecatingly, blue head drooping, and blue tail between blue legs, making abject apologies for his horrible condition. But Henry had done his work well. They stood around in rapt admiration.

"Blue dog," said the showman, walking forward proudly and stumbling violently over the cords of the dressing-gown. "Blue dog," he repeated, recovering his balance and removing the tinsel crown from his nose to his brow. "You never saw a blue dog before, did you? No, and you aren't likely to see one again, neither. It was made blue special for this show. It's the only blue dog in the world. Folks'll be comin' from all over the world to see this blue dog—an' thrown in in a penny show! If it was in the Zoo you'd have to pay a shilling to see it, I bet. It's—it's jus' luck for you it's here. I guess the folks at the Zoo wish they'd got it. Tain't many shows have blue dogs. Brown an' black an' white—but not blue. Why, folks pay money jus' to see shows of ornery dogs—so you're jus' lucky to see a blue dog *an'* a dead bear from Russia *an'* a giant, *an'* a wild cat, *an'* a China rat for jus' one penny."

After each speech William had to remove from his mouth the rug fringe which persisted in obeying the force of gravity rather than William's idea of what a moustache should be.

"It's jus' paint. Henry's gate's being painted blue," said one critic feebly, but on the whole the Outlaws had scored a distinct success in the blue dog.

Then, while they stood in silent admiration round the unhappy animal, came a sound from the next door, a gentle sound like the sighing of the wind through the trees. It rose and fell. It rose again and fell again. It increased in volume with each repetition, till at its height it sounded like a wild animal in pain.

"What's that?" asked the audience breathlessly.

William was slightly uneasy. He was not sure whether this fresh development would add lustre or dishonour to his show.

"Yes," he said darkly to gain time, "what is it? I guess you'd like to know what it is!"

"Garn! It's jus' snorin'."

"Snorin'!" repeated William. "It's not ornery snorin', that isn't. Jus' listen, that's all! You couldn't snore like that, I bet. Huh!"

They listened spellbound to the gentle sound, growing louder and louder till at its loudest it brought rapt smiles to their faces, then ceasing abruptly, then silence. Then again the gentle sound that grew and grew.

William asked Henry in a stage whisper if they oughtn't to charge extra for listening to it. The audience hastily explained that they weren't listening, they "jus' couldn't help hearin'."

A second batch of sightseers had arrived and were paying their entrance pennies, but the first batch refused to move. William, emboldened by success, opened the door and they crept out to the landing and listened with ears pressed to the magic door.

Henry now did the honours of showman. William stood, majestic in his glorious apparel, deep in thought. Then to his face came the faint smile that Inspiration brings to her votaries. He ordered the audience back into the showroom and shut the door. Then he took off his shoes and softly and with bated breath opened Aunt Emily's door and peeped within. It was rather a close afternoon, and she lay on her bed on the top of her eiderdown. She had slipped off her skirt so as not to crush it, and she lay in her immense stature in a blouse and striped petticoat, while from her open mouth issued the fascinating sounds. In sleep Aunt Emily was not beautiful.

William thoughtfully propped up a cushion in the doorway and stood considering the situation.

In a few minutes the showroom was filled with a silent, expectant crowd. In a corner near the door was a new notice:

> PLACE FOR TAKING
> OFF SHOES AND TAKING
> OTH OF SILENCE

William, after administering the oath of silence to a select party in his most impressive manner, led them shoeless and on tiptoe to the next room.

Over Aunt Emily's bed hung another notice:

> FAT WILD WOMAN
> TORKIN NATIF
> LANGWIDGE

They stood in a hushed, delighted group around her bed. The sounds never ceased, never abated. William only allowed them two minutes in the room. They came out reluctantly, paid more money, joined the end of the queue and re-entered. More and more children came to see the show, but the show now consisted solely in Aunt Emily.

The China rat had licked off all its stripes; Smuts was fast asleep; Ginger was sitting down on the seat of a chair and Douglas on the back of it and Ginger had insisted at last on air and sight and had put his head out where the two sheets joined; the Russian Bear had fallen on to the floor and no one had picked it up; Chips lay in a disconsolate heap, a victim of acute melancholia—and no one cared for any of these things. Newcomers passed by them hurriedly and stood shoeless in the queue outside Aunt Emily's room eagerly awaiting their turn. Those who came out simply went to the end again to wait another turn. Many returned home for more money, for Aunt Emily was 1d extra and each visit after the first, ½d. The Sunday School bell pealed forth its summons, but no one left the show. The vicar was depressed that evening. The attendance at Sunday School had been the worst on record. And still Aunt Emily slept and snored with a rapt, silent crowd around her. But William could never rest content. He possessed ambition that would have put many of his elders to shame. He cleared the room and re-opened it after a few minutes, during which his clients waited in breathless suspense.

When they re-entered there was a fresh exhibit. William's keen eye had been searching out each detail of the room. On the table by her bed now stood a glass containing teeth that William had discovered on the washstand, and a switch of hair and a toothless comb that William had discovered on the dressing-table. These all bore notices:

FAT WILD WOMAN'S TEETH	FAT WILD WOMAN'S HARE	FAT WILD WOMAN'S KOME

Were it not that the slightest noise meant instant expulsion from the show (some of their number had already suffered that bitter fate) there would have been no restraining the audience. As it was, they crept in, silent, expectant, thrilled, to watch and listen for the blissful two minutes. And Aunt Emily never failed them. Still she slept and snored. They borrowed money recklessly from each other. The poor sold their dearest treasures to the rich, and still they came again and again. And still Aunt Emily slept and snored. It would be interesting to know how long this would have gone on, had she not, on the top note of a peal that was a pure delight to her audience, awakened with a start and glanced around her. At first she thought that the cluster of small boys around her was a dream, especially as they turned and fled precipitately at once. Then she sat up and her eyes fell upon the table by her bed, the notices, and finally upon the petrified horror-stricken showman. She sprang up and, seizing him by the shoulders, shook him till his teeth chattered, the tinsel crown fell down, encircling ears and nose, and one of his moustaches fell limply at his feet.

"You wicked boy!" she said as she shook him, "you *wicked, wicked, wicked* boy!"

He escaped from her grasp and fled to the showroom, where, in sheer self-defence, he moved a table and three chairs across the door. The room was empty except for Henry, the blue dog and the still sleeping Smuts. All that was left of the giant was the crumpled sheets. Douglas had snatched up his rat as he fled. The last of their clients was seen scrambling along the top of the garden wall on all fours with all possible speed.

Mechanically William straightened his crown.

"She's woke," he said. "She's mad wild."

He listened apprehensively for angry footsteps descending the stairs and his father's dread summons, but none came. Aunt Emily could be heard moving about in her room, but that was all. A wild hope came to him that, given a little time, she might forget the incident.

"Let's count the money—" said Henry at last.

They counted.

"Seven-an'-six!" screamed William. "Seven-an'-six! Jolly good, I *should* say! An' it would only have been about two shillings without Aunt Emily, an' I thought of her, didn't I? I guess you can all be jolly grateful to me."

"All right," said Henry unkindly. "I'm not envying you, am I? You're welcome to it when she tells your father."

And William's proud spirits dropped.

Then came the opening of the fateful door and heavy steps descending the stairs.

William's mother had returned from her weekly visit to her friend. She was placing her umbrella in the stand as Aunt Emily, hatted and coated and carrying a bag, descended. William's father had just awakened from his peaceful Sunday afternoon slumber and, hearing his wife, had come into the hall.

Aunt Emily fixed her eye upon him and said:

"Will you be good enough to procure a conveyance? After the indignities to which I have been subjected in this house I refuse to remain in it a moment longer."

Quivering with indignation she gave details of the indignities to which she had been subjected. William's mother pleaded, apologised, coaxed. William's father went quietly out to telephone for a taxi. When it arrived she was still talking in the hall.

"A crowd of vulgar little boys," she was saying, "and horrible, indecent placards all over the room."

Mr. Brown carried her bag down to the cab.

"And me in my state of health," she said as she followed him. From the cab she gave her parting shot.

"And if this horrible thing hadn't happened, I might have stayed with you all the winter and perhaps part of the spring."

William's father wiped his brow with his handkerchief as the cab drove off.

"How dreadful!" said his wife, but she avoided meeting his eye. "It's—it's *disgraceful* of William," she went on with sudden spirit. "You must speak to him."

"I will," said his father determinedly. "William!" he shouted sternly from the hall.

William's heart sank.

"She's told," he murmured, his last hope gone.

"You'd better go and get it over," advised Henry.

"William!" repeated the voice still more fiercely.

Henry moved nearer the window, prepared for instant flight if the voice's owner should follow it up the stairs.

"Go on," he urged. "He'll only come up for you."

William slowly removed the barricade and descended the stairs. He had remembered to take off the crown and dressing-gown, but his one-sided moustache still hung limply over his mouth.

His father was standing in the hall.

"What's that horrible thing on your face?" he began.

"Whiskers," answered William laconically.

His father accepted the explanation.

"Is it true," he went on, "that you actually took your friends into your aunt's room without permission and hung vulgar placards around it?"

William glanced up into his father's face and suddenly took hope. Mr. Brown was no actor.

"Yes," he admitted.

"It's disgraceful," said Mr. Brown, "*disgraceful*! That's all."

But it was not quite all. Something hard and round slipped into William's hand. He ran lightly upstairs.

"Hello!" said Henry, surprised. "That's not taken long. What—"

William opened his hand and showed something that shone upon his extended palm.

"Look!" he said. "Crumbs! Look!" It was a bright half-crown.

CHAPTER 6

A QUESTION OF GRAMMAR

IT was raining. It had been raining all morning. William was intensely bored with his family.

"What can I do?" he demanded of his father for the tenth time.

"*Nothing!*" said his father fiercely from behind his newspaper.

William followed his mother into the kitchen.

"What can I do?" he said plaintively.

"Couldn't you just sit quietly?" suggested his mother.

"That's not *doin'* anything," William said. "I *could* sit quietly all day," he went on aggressively, "if I wanted."

"But you never do."

"No, 'cause there wouldn't be any *sense* in it, would there?"

"Couldn't you read or draw or something?"

"No, that's lessons. That's not doin' anything!"

"I could teach you to knit if you like."

With one crushing glance, William left her.

He went to the drawing-room, where his sister Ethel was knitting a jumper and talking to a friend.

"And I heard her say to him——" she was saying. She broke off with the sigh of a patient martyr as William came in. He sat down and glared at her. She exchanged a glance of resigned exasperation with her friend.

"What are you doing, William?" said the friend sweetly.

"Nothin'," said William with a scowl.

"Shut the door after you when you go out, won't you, William?" said Ethel equally sweetly.

83

William at that insult rose with dignity and went to the door. At the door he turned.

"I wun't stay here now," he said with slow contempt, "not even if—even if—even if," he paused to consider the most remote contingency, "not even if you wanted me," he said at last emphatically.

He shut the door behind him and his expression relaxed into a sardonic smile.

"I bet they feel *small*!" he said to the umbrella-stand.

He went upstairs, where his nineteen-year-old brother Robert was showing off his new camera to a friend.

"You see—" he was saying, then, catching sight of William, "Oh, get out!"

William got out.

He returned to his mother in the kitchen with a still more jaundiced view of life. It was still raining. His mother was doing the household accounts.

"Can I go out?" he said gloomily.

"No, of course not. It's pouring."

"I don't mind rain."

"Don't be silly."

William considered that few boys in the whole world were handicapped by more unsympathetic parents than he.

"Why," he said pathetically, "have they got friends in an' me not?"

"I suppose you didn't think of asking anyone," she said calmly.

"Well, can I have someone now?"

"No, it's too late," said Mrs. Brown, raising her head from the butcher's bill and murmuring "ten-and-eleven-pence" to herself.

"Well, when can I?"

She raised a harassed face.

"William, do be quiet! Any time, if you ask. Eighteen-and-twopence."

"Can I have lots?"

"Oh, go and ask your father."

William went out.

He returned to the dining-room, where his father was still reading a paper. The sigh with which his father greeted his entrance was not one of relief.

"If you've come to ask questions—" he began threateningly.

"I haven't," said William quickly. "Father, when you're all away on Saturday, can I have a party?"

"No, of course not," said his father irritably. "Can't you *do* something?"

William, goaded to desperation, burst into a flood of eloquence.

"The sort of things I want to do they don't want me to do an' the sort of things I don't want to do they want me to do. Mother said to knit. *Knit!*"

His scorn and fury were indescribable. His father looked out of the window.

"Thank Heavens, it's stopped raining! Go out!"

William went out.

There were some quite interesting things to do outside. In the road there were puddles, and the sensation of walking through a puddle, as every boy knows, is a very pleasant one. The hedges, when shaken, sent quite a shower-bath upon the shaker, which also is a pleasant sensation. The ditch was full and there was the thrill of seeing how often one could jump across it without going in. One went in more often than not. It is also fascinating to walk in mud, scraping it along with one's boots. William's spirits rose, but he could not shake off the idea of the party. Quite suddenly he wanted to have a party and he wanted to have it on Saturday. His family would be away on Saturday. They were going to spend the day with an aunt. Aunts rarely included William in their invitation.

He came home wet and dirty and cheerful. He approached his father warily.

"Did you say I could have a party, Father?" he said casually.

"*No*, I did *not*," said Mr. Brown firmly.

William let the matter rest for the present.

He spent most of the English Grammar class in school next morning considering it. There was a great deal to be said for a party in the absence of one's parents and grown-up brother and sister. He'd like to ask George and Ginger and Henry and Douglas and—and—and—heaps of them. He'd like to ask them all. "They" were the whole class—thirty in number.

"What have I just been saying, William?"

William sighed. That was the foolish sort of question that schoolmistresses were always asking. They ought to know themselves what they'd just been saying better than anyone. *He* never knew. Why were they always asking him? He looked blank. Then:

"Was it anythin' about participles?" He remembered something vaguely about participles, but it mightn't have been to-day.

Miss Jones groaned.

"That was ever so long ago, William," she said. "You've not been attending."

William cleared his throat with a certain dignity and made no answer.

"Tell him, Henry."

Henry ceased his enthralling occupation of trying to push a fly into his ink-well with his nib and answered mechanically:

"Two negatives make an affirmative."

"Yes. Say that, William."

William repeated it without betraying any great interest in the fact.

"Yes. What's a negative, William?"

William sighed.

"Something about photographs?" he said obligingly.

"*No*," snapped Miss Jones. She found William and the heat (William particularly) rather trying.

"It's 'no' and 'not.' And an affirmative is 'yes.' "

"Oh," said William politely.

"So two 'nos' and 'nots' mean 'yes,' if they're in the same sentence. If you said 'There's not no money in the box,' you mean there is."

William considered.

He said "Oh" again.

Then he seemed suddenly to become intelligent.

"Then," he said, "if you say 'no' and 'not' in the same sentence does it mean 'yes'?"

"Certainly."

William smiled.

William's smile was a rare thing.

"Thank you," he said.

Miss Jones was quite touched. "It's all right, William," she said, "I'm glad you're beginning to take an interest in your work."

William was murmuring to himself:

" 'No, of course *not*,' and 'No, I did not,' and a 'no' an' a 'not' mean a 'yes,' so he meant 'yes, of course,' and 'yes, I did.' "

He waited till the Friday before he gave his invitations with a casual air.

"My folks is goin' away to-morrow an' they said I could have a few fren's in to tea. Can you come? Tell your mother they said jus' to come an' not bother to write."

He was a born strategist. Not one of his friends' parents guessed the true state of affairs. When William's conscience (that curious organ) rose to reproach him, he said to it firmly:

"He *said* I could. He said '*Yes*, of course.' He said '*Yes*, I did.' "

He asked them *all*. He thought that while you are having a party you might as well have a big one. He hinted darkly at unrestrained joy and mirth. They all accepted the invitation.

William's mother took an anxious farewell of him on Saturday morning.

"You don't mind being left, darling, do you?"

"No, Mother," said William with perfect truth.

"You won't do anything we've told you not to, will you?"

"No, Mother. Only things you've said 'yes' to."

Cook and Jane had long looked forward to this day. There would be very little to do in the house and as far as William was concerned they hoped for the best.

William was out all the morning. At lunch he was ominously quiet and polite. Jane decided to go with her young man to the pictures.

Cook said she didn't mind being left, as "that Master William" had gone out and there seemed to be no prospect of his return before tea-time.

So Jane went to the pictures.

About three o'clock the postman came and cook went to the door for the letters. Then she stood gazing down the road as though transfixed.

William had collected his guests en route. He was bringing them joyfully home with him. Clean and starched and prim had they issued from their homes, but they had grown hilarious under William's benign influence. They had acquired sticks and stones and old tins from the ditches as they came along. They perceived from William's general attitude towards it that it was no ordinary party. They were a happy crowd. William headed them with a trumpet.

They trooped in at the garden gate. Cook, pale and speechless, watched them. Then her speechlessness departed.

"You're not coming in here!" she said fiercely. "Why've you brought all those boys cluttering up the garden?"

"They've come to tea," said William calmly.

She grew paler still.

"That they've *not*!" she said fiercely. "What your father'd say—"

"He *said* they could come," said William. "I asked him an' he said 'Yes, of course,' an' I asked if he'd said so an'

88

he said 'Yes, I did.' That's what he said 'cause of English Grammar an' wot Miss Jones said."

Cook's answer was to slam the door in his face and lock it. The thirty guests were slightly disconcerted, but not for long.

"Come on!" shouted William excitedly. "She's the enemy. Let's storm her ole castle."

The guests' spirits rose. This promised to be infinitely superior to the usual party.

They swarmed round to the back of the house. The enemy had bolted the back door and was fastening all the windows. Purple with fury, she shook her fist at William through the drawing-room window. William brandished his piece of stick and blew his trumpet in defiant reply. The army had armed itself with every kind of weapon, including the raspberry-canes whose careful placing was the result of a whole day's work by William's father. William decided to climb up to the balcony outside Ethel's open bedroom window with the help of his noble band. The air was full of their defiant war-whoops. They filled the front garden, trampling on all the rose-beds, cheering William as he swarmed up to the balcony, his trumpet between his lips. The enemy appeared at the window and shut it with a bang, and William, startled, dropped down among his followers. They raised a hoarse roar of anger.

"Mean ole cat!" shouted the enraged general.

The blood of the army was up. No army of thirty strong worthy of its name could ever consent to be worsted by an enemy of one. All the doors and windows were bolted. There was only one thing to be done. And this the general did, encouraged by loyal cheers from his army. "Go it, ole William! Yah! He—oo—o!"

The stone with which William broke the drawing-room window fell upon a small occasional table, scattering Mrs. Brown's cherished silver far and wide.

William, with the born general's contempt for the minor devastations of war, enlarged the hole and helped his

89

gallant band through with only a limited number of cuts and scratches. They were drunk with the thrill of battle. They left the garden with its wreck of rose-trees and its trampled lawn and crowded through the broken window with imminent danger to life and limb. The enemy was shutting the small window of the coal-cellar, and there William imprisoned her, turning the key with a loud yell of triumph.

The party then proceeded.

It fulfilled the expectations of the guests that it was to be a party unlike any other party. At other parties they played "Hide and Seek"—with smiling but firm mothers and aunts and sisters stationed at intervals with damping effects upon one's spirits, with "not in the bedrooms, dear," and "mind the umbrella-stand," and "certainly not in the drawing-room," and "don't shout so loud, darling." But this was Hide and Seek from the realms of perfection. Up the stairs and down the stairs, in all the bedrooms, sliding down the banisters, in and out of the drawing-room, leaving trails of muddy boots and shattered ornaments as they went!

Ginger found a splendid hiding-place in Robert's bed, where his boots left a perfect impression of their muddy soles in several places. Henry found another in Ethel's wardrobe, crouching upon her satin evening shoes among her evening dresses. George banged the drawing-room door with such violence that the handle came off in his hand. Douglas became entangled in the dining-room curtain, which yielded to his struggles and descended upon him and an old china bowl upon the sideboard. It was such a party as none of them had dreamed of; it was bliss undiluted. The house was full of shouting and yelling, of running to and fro of small boys mingled with subterranean murmurs of cook's rage. Cook was uttering horrible imprecations and hurling lumps of coal at the door. She was Irish and longed to return to the fray.

It was William who discovered first that it was tea-time and there was no tea. At first he felt slightly aggrieved.

Then he thought of the larder and his spirits rose.

"Come on!" he called. "All jus' get what you can."

They trooped in, panting, shouting, laughing, and all just got what they could.

Ginger seized the remnants of a cold ham and picked the bone, George with great gusto drank a whole jar of cream, William and Douglas between them ate a gooseberry pie, Henry ate a whole currant cake. Each foraged for himself. They ate two bowls of cold vegetables, a joint of cold beef, two pots of honey, three dozen oranges, three loaves and two pots of dripping. They experimented upon lard, onions and raw sausages. They left the larder a place of gaping emptiness. Meanwhile cook's voice, growing hoarser and hoarser as the result of the inhalation of coal dust and exhalation of imprecations, still arose from the depths, and still the door of the coal-cellar shook and rattled.

Then one of the guests who had been at the drawing-room window came back.

"She's coming home!" he shouted excitedly.

They flocked to the window.

Jane was bidding a fond farewell to her young man at the side gate.

"Don't let her come in!" yelled William. "Come on!"

With a smile of blissful reminiscence upon her face, Jane turned in at the gate. She was totally unprepared for being met by a shower of missiles from upper windows.

A lump of lard hit her on the ear and knocked her hat on to one side. She retreated hastily to the side gate.

"Go on! Send her into the road."

A shower of onions, the ham bone, and a few potatoes pursued her into the road. Shouts of triumph rent the air. Then the shouts of triumph died away abruptly. William's smile also faded away, and his hand, in the act of flinging an onion, dropped. A cab was turning in at the front gate. In the sudden silence that fell upon the party, cook's hoarse cries for vengeance rose with redoubled force from the coal-cellar. William grew pale.

The cab contained his family.

Two hours later a small feminine friend of William's who had called with a note for his mother, looked up to William's window and caught sight of William's untidy head.

"Come and play with me, William," she called eagerly.

"I can't. I'm goin' to bed," said William sternly.

"Why? Are you ill, William?"

"No."

"Well, why are you going to bed, William?"

William leant out of the window.

"I'm goin' to bed," he said, " 'cause my father don't understand 'bout English Grammar, that's why!"

CHAPTER 7

THE OUTLAWS

IT was a half-holiday and William was in his bedroom making careful preparations for the afternoon. On the mantelpiece stood in readiness half a cake (the result of a successful raid on the larder) and a bottle of licorice water. This beverage was made by shaking up a piece of licorice in water. It was much favoured by the band of Outlaws to which William belonged and which met secretly every half-holiday in a disused barn about a quarter of a mile from William's house.

So far the Outlaws had limited their activities to wrestling matches, adventure seeking, and culinary operations. The week before, they had cooked two sausages which William had taken from the larder on cook's night out and had conveyed to the barn beneath his shirt and next his skin. Perhaps "cooked" is too euphemistic a term. To be quite accurate, they had held the sausages over a smoking fire till completely blackened, and then consumed the charred remains with the utmost relish.

William put the bottle of licorice water in one pocket and the half cake in another and was preparing to leave the house in his usual stealthy fashion—through the bathroom window, down the scullery roof, and down the water-pipe to the back garden. Even when unencumbered by the presence of a purloined half cake, William infinitely preferred this mode of exit to the simpler one of walking out of the front door. As he came out on to the landing, however, he heard the sound of the opening and shutting of the hall door and of exuberant greetings in the hall.

"Oh! I'm *so* glad you've come, dear. And is this the baby! The *duck*! Well, den, how's 'oo, den? Go—o—oo."

This was William's mother.

"Oh, crumbs!" said William, and retreated hastily. He sat down on his bed to wait till the coast was clear. Soon came the sound of footsteps ascending the stairs.

"Oh, William," said his mother, as she entered his room, "Mrs. Butler's come with her baby to spend the afternoon, and we'd arranged to go out till tea-time with the baby, but she's got such a headache, I'm insisting on her lying down for the afternoon in the drawing-room. But she's *so* worried about the baby not getting out this nice afternoon."

"Oh!" said William, without interest.

"Well, cook's out and Emma has to get the tea and answer the door, and Ethel's away, and I told Mrs. Butler I was *sure* you wouldn't mind taking the baby out for a bit in the perambulator!"

William stared at her, speechless. The Medusa's classic expression of horror was as nothing to William's at that moment. Then he moistened his lips and spoke in a hoarse voice.

"*Me?*" he said. "*Me? Me* take a baby out in a pram?"

"Well, dear," said his mother deprecatingly, "I know it's your half-holiday, but you'd be out of doors getting the fresh air, which is the great thing. It's a nice baby and a nice pram and not heavy to push, and Mrs. Butler would be *so* grateful to you."

"Yes, I should think she'd be that," said William bitterly. "She'd have a right to be that if I took the baby out in a pram."

"Now, William, I'm sure you'd like to help, and I'm sure you wouldn't like your father to hear that you wouldn't even do a little thing like that for poor Mrs. Butler. And she's got such a headache."

"*A little thing like that!*" repeated William out of the bitterness of his soul.

94

But the Fates were closing round him. He was aware that he would know no peace till he had done the horrible thing demanded of him. Sorrowfully and reluctantly he bowed to the inevitable.

"All right," he muttered, "I'll be down in a minute."

He heard them fussing over the baby in the hall. Then he heard his elder brother's voice.

"You surely don't mean to say, Mother," Robert was saying with the crushing superiority of nineteen years, "that you're going to trust that child to—William."

"Well," said William's mother, "someone has to take him out. It's such a lovely afternoon. I'm sure it's very kind of William, on his half-holiday too. And she's got *such* a headache."

"Well, of course," said Robert in the voice of one who washes his hands of all further responsibility, "you know William as well as I do."

"Oh, dear!" sighed William's mother. "And everything so nicely settled, Robert, and you must come and find fault with it all. If you don't want William to take him out, will you take him out yourself?"

Robert retreated hastily to the dining-room and continued the conversation from a distance.

"I don't want to take him out myself—thanks very much, all the same! All I say is—you know William as well as I do. I'm not finding fault with anything. I am simply stating a fact."

Then William came downstairs.

"Here he is, dear, all ready for you, and you needn't go far away—just up and down the road, if you like, but stay out till tea-time. He's a dear little baby, isn't he? And isn't it a nice Willy-Billy den, to take it out a nice ta-ta, while its mummy goes bye-byes, den?"

William blushed for pure shame.

He pushed the pram down o the end of the road and round the corner. In comparison with William's feelings, the feelings of some of the early martyrs must have been pure bliss. A nice way for an Outlaw to spend the afternoon! He dreaded to meet any of his brother-outlaws, yet, irresistibly and as a magnet, their meeting-place attracted him. He wheeled the pram off the road and down the country lane towards the field which held their sacred barn. He stopped at the stile that led into the field and gazed wistfully across to the barn in the distance. The infant sat and sucked its thumb and stared at him. Finally it began to converse.

"Blab — blab — blab — blab — blub — blub — blub!"

"Oh, you shut up!" said William crushingly.

Annoyed at the prolonged halt, it seized its pram cover, pulled it off its hooks, and threw it into the road. While William was picking it up, it threw the pillow on to his head. Then it chuckled. William began to conceive an active dislike of it. Suddenly the Great Idea came to him. His face cleared. He took a piece of string from his pocket and tied the pram carefully to the railings. Then, lifting the baby cautiously and gingerly out, he climbed the stile with it and set off across the fields towards the barn. He held the baby to his chest with both arms clasped tightly round its waist. Its feet dangled in the air. It occupied the time by kicking William in the stomach, pulling his hair, and putting its fingers in his eyes.

"It beats me," panted William to himself, "what people see in babies! Scratchin' an' kickin' and blindin' folks and pullin' their hair all out!"

When he entered the barn he was greeted by a sudden silence.

"Look here!" began one Outlaw in righteous indignation.

"It's a kidnap," said William triumphantly. "We'll get a ransom on it."

They gazed at him in awed admiration. This was surely the cream of outlawry. He set the infant on the ground, where it toddled for a few steps and sat down suddenly and violently. It then stared fixedly at the tallest boy present and smiled seraphically.

"Dad—dad—dad—dad—dad!"

Douglas, the tallest boy, grinned sheepishly. "It thinks I'm its father," he explained complacently to the company.

"Well," said Henry, who was William's rival for the leadership of the Outlaws, "what do we do first? That's the question."

"In books," said the Outlaw called Ginger, "they write a note to its people and say they want a ransom."

"We won't do that—not just yet," said William hastily.

"Well, it's not much sense holdin' somethin' up to ransom and not tellin' the folks that they've got to pay nor nothin', is it?" said Ginger with the final air of a man whose logic is unassailable.

"N—oo," said William. "But—" with a gleam of hope—"who's got a paper and pencil? I'm simply statin' a fact. Who's got a paper and pencil?"

No one spoke.

"Oh, yes!" went on William in triumph. "Go on! Write a note. Write a note without paper and pencil, and we'll all watch. Huh!"

"Well," said Ginger sulkily, "I don't s'pose they had paper and pencils in outlaw days. They weren't invented. They wrote on—on—on leaves or something," he ended vaguely.

"Well, go on. Write on leaves," said William still more triumphant. "We're not stoppin' you, are we? I'm simply statin' a fact. Write on leaves."

They were interrupted by a yell of pain from Douglas. Flattered by the parental relations so promptly established by the baby, he had ventured to make its further acquaintance. With vague memories of his mother's treatment of infants, he had inserted a finger in its mouth. The infant happened to possess four front teeth, two upper and two lower, and they closed like a vice upon Douglas's finger. He was now examining the marks.

"Look! Right deep down! See it? Wotcher think of that! Nearly to the bone! Pretty savage baby you've brought along," he said to William.

"I jolly well know that," said William feelingly. "It's your own fault for touching it. It's all right if you leave it alone. Just don't touch it, that's all. Anyway, it's mine, and I never said you could go fooling about with it, did I? It wouldn't bite *me*, I bet!"

"Well, what about the ransom?" persisted Henry.

"Someone can go and tell its people and bring back the ransom," suggested Ginger.

There was a short silence. Then Douglas took his injured finger from his mouth and asked pertinently:

"Who?"

"William brought it," suggested Henry.

"Yes, so I bet I've done my share."

"Well, what's anyone else goin' to do, I'd like to know? Go round to every house in this old place and ask if they've had a baby taken off them and if they'd pay a ransom for it back? That's sense, isn't it? You know where you got it from, don't you, and you can go and get its ransom?"

"I can, but I'm not goin' to," said William finally. "I'm simply statin' a fact. I'm not goin' to. And if anyone says I daren't" (glancing round pugnaciously), "I'll fight 'em for it."

No one said he daren't. The fact was too patent to need stating. Henry hastily changed the subject.

"Anyway, what have we brought for the feast?"

William produced his licorice water and half cake, Douglas two slices of raw ham and a dog biscuit, Ginger some popcorn and some cold boiled potatoes wrapped up in newspaper, Henry a cold apple dumpling and a small bottle of paraffin-oil.

"I knew the wood would be wet after the rain. It's to make the fire burn. That's sense, isn't it?"

"Only one thing to cook," said Ginger sadly, looking at the slices of ham.

"We can cook up the potatoes and the dumpling. They don't look half enough cooked. Let's put them on the floor here and go out for adventures first. All different ways and back in a quarter of an hour."

The Outlaws generally spent part of the afternoon dispersed in search of adventure. So far they had wooed the Goddess of Danger chiefly by trespassing on the ground of irascible farmers in hopes of a chase which were generally fulfilled.

They deposited their store on the ground in a corner of the barn, and with a glance at the "kidnap," who was seated happily upon the floor engaged in chewing its hat-strings, they went out, carefully closing the door.

After a quarter of an hour Ginger and William arrived at the door simultaneously from opposite directions.

"Any luck?"

"No."

"Same here. Let's start the old fire going."

They opened the door and went in. The infant was sitting on the floor among the stores, or rather among what was left of the stores. There was paraffin-oil on its hair, face, arms, frock and feet. It was drenched in paraffin-oil. The empty bottle and its hat lay by its side. Mingled with the paraffin-oil all over its person was cold boiled potato. It was holding the apple dumpling in its hand.

"Ball!" it announced ecstatically from behind its mask of potato and paraffin-oil.

They stood in silence for a minute. Then, "Who's going to make that fire burn now?" said Ginger, glaring at the empty bottle.

"Yes," said William slowly, "an' who's goin' to take that baby home? I'm simply statin' a fact. Who's goin' to take that baby home?"

There was no doubt that when William condescended to adopt a phrase from any of his family's vocabularies, he considerably overworked it.

"Well, it did it itself. It's no one else's fault, is it?"

"No, it's not," said William. "But that's the sort of thing folks never see. Anyway, I'm goin' to wash its face."

"What with?"

William took out his grimy handkerchief and advanced upon his prey. His bottle of licorice water was lying untouched in the corner. He took out the cork.

"Goin' to wash it in that dirty stuff?"

"It's made of water—clean water—I made it myself, so I bet I ought to know, oughtn't I? That's what folks wash in, isn't it?—clean water?"

"Yes," bitterly, "and what are we goin' to drink, I'd like to know? You'd think that baby had got enough of our stuff—our potatoes and our apple dumpling, an' our oil—without you goin' an' givin' it our licorice water as well."

William was passing his handkerchief, moistened with licorice water, over the surface of the baby's face. The baby had caught a corner of it firmly between its teeth and refused to release it.

"If you'd got to take this baby home like this," he said, "you wouldn't be thinking much about drinking licorice water. I'm simply statin'—"

"Oh, shut up saying that!" said Ginger in sudden exasperation. "I'm sick of it."

At that moment the door was flung open and in walked slowly a large cow closely followed by Henry and Douglas.

Henry's face was one triumphant beam. He felt that his prestige, eclipsed by William's kidnapping coup, was restored.

"I've brought a cow," he announced, "fetched it all the way from Farmer Litton's field—five fields off, too, an' it took some fetching too."

"Well, what for?" said William after a moment's silence.

Henry gave a superior laugh.

"What for! You've not read much about outlaws, I guess. They always drove in cattle from the surroundin' districks."

"Well, what for?" said William again, giving a tug at his handkerchief, which the infant still refused to release.

"Well—er—well—to kill an' roast, I suppose," said Henry lamely.

"Well, go on," said William. "Kill it an' roast it. We're not stoppin' you, are we? Kill it an' roast it—an' get hung for murder. I s'pose it's murder to kill cows same as it is to kill people—'cept for butchers."

The cow advanced slowly and warily towards the "kidnap," who promptly dropped the handkerchief and beamed with joy.

"Bow—wow!" it said excitedly.

"Anyway, let's get on with the feast," said Douglas.

"Feast!" echoed Ginger bitterly. "Feast! Not much feast left! That baby William brought's used all the paraffin-oil and potatoes, and it's squashed the apple dumpling, and William's washed its face in the licorice water."

Henry gazed at it dispassionately and judicially.

"Yes—it looks like as if someone had washed it in licorice water—and as if it had used up all the oil and potatoes. It doesn't look like as if it would fetch much ransom. You seem to have pretty well mucked it up."

"Oh, shut up about the baby," said William, picking up his damp and now prune-coloured handkerchief. "I'm just about sick of it. Come on with the fire."

They made a little pile of twigs in the field and began the process of lighting it.

"I hope that cow won't hurt the 'kidnap,' " said Douglas suddenly. "Go and see, William; it's your kidnap."

"Well, an' it's Henry's cow, and I'm sorry for that cow if it tries playin' tricks on that baby."

But he rose from his knees reluctantly and threw open the barn door. The cow and the baby were still gazing admiringly at each other. From the cow's mouth at the end of a long, sodden ribbon, hung the chewed remains of the baby's hat. The baby was holding up the dog biscuit and crowed delightfully as the cow bent down its head and cautiously and gingerly smelt it. As William entered, the cow turned round and switched its tail against the baby's head. At the piercing howl that followed, the whole band of Outlaws entered the barn.

"What are you doing to the poor little thing?" said Douglas to William.

"It's Henry's cow," said William despairingly. "It hit it. Oh, go on, shut up! Do shut up!"

The howls redoubled.

"You brought it," said Henry accusingly, raising his voice to be heard above the baby's fury and indignation. "Can't you stop it? Not much sense taking babies about if you don't know how to stop 'em crying!"

The baby was now purple in the face.

The Outlaws stood around and watched it helplessly.

"P'raps it's hungry," suggested Douglas.

He took up the half cake from the remains of the stores and held it out tentatively to the baby. The baby stopped crying suddenly.

"Dad—dad—dad—dad—dad," it said tearfully.

Douglas blushed and grinned.

"Keeps on thinking I'm its father," he said with conscious superiority. "Here, like some cake?"

The baby broke off a handful and conveyed it to its mouth.

"It's eating it," cried Douglas in shrill excitement. After thoroughly masticating it, however, the baby repented of its condescension and ejected the mouthful in several instalments.

William blushed for it.

"Oh, come on, let's go and look at the fire," he said weakly.

They left the barn and returned to the scene of the fire-lighting. The cow, still swinging the remains of the baby's hat from its mouth, was standing with its front feet firmly planted on the remains of what had been a promising fire.

"Look!" cried William in undisguised pleasure. "Look at Henry's cow! Pretty nice sort of cow you've brought, Henry. Not much sense taking cows about if you can't stop them puttin' folks' fires out."

After a heated argument, the Outlaws turned their

attention to the cow. The cow refused to be "shoo'd off."
It simply stood immovable and stared them out. Ginger
approached cautiously and gave it a little push. It switched
its tail into his eye and continued to munch the baby's hat-
string. Upon William's approaching it lowered its head,
and William retreated hastily. At last they set off to collect
some fresh wood and light a fresh fire. Soon they were
blissfully consuming two blackened slices of ham, the popcorn, and what was left of the cake.

After the "feast," Ginger and William, as Wild Indians,
attacked the barn, which was defended by Douglas and
Henry. The "kidnap" crawled round inside on all fours,
picking up any treasures it might come across en route and
testing their effect on its palate.

Occasionally it carried on a conversation with its defen-
ders, bringing with it a strong perfume of paraffin-oil as it
approached.

"Blab — blab — blab — blab — blub — blub — Dad
—dad—dad—dad—dad. Go—o—o—o."

William had insisted on a place on the attacking side.

"I couldn't put any feelin'," he explained, "into fightin'
for that baby."

When they finally decided to set off homewards, William
gazed hopelessly at his charge. Its appearance defied des-
cription. For many years afterwards William associated
babies in his mind with paraffin-oil and potato.

"Just help me get the potato out of its hair," he pleaded;
"never mind the oil and the rest of it."

"My hat! doesn't it smell funny!—and doesn't it look
funny—all oil and potato and bits of cake!" said Ginger.

"Oh! shut up about it," said William irritably.

The cow followed them down to the stile and watched
them stolidly as they climbed it.

"Bow—wow!" murmured the baby in affectionate farewell.

William looked round for the pram, but—the pram was
gone—only the piece of string dangled from the railings.

"Crumbs!" said William. "Talk about bad luck! I'm simply statin' a fact. Talk about bad luck!"

At that minute the pram appeared, charging down the hill at full speed with a cargo of small boys. At the bottom of the hill it overturned into a ditch, accompanied by its cargo. To judge from its appearance, it had passed the afternoon performing the operation.

"That's my pram!" said William to the cargo, as it emerged, joyfully, from the ditch.

"Garn! S'ours! We found it."

"Well, I left it there."

"Come on! We'll fight for it," said Ginger, rolling up his sleeves in a business-like manner. The other Outlaws followed his example. The pram's cargo eyed them appraisingly.

"Oh, all right! Take your rotten old pram!" they said at last.

Douglas placed the baby in its seat and William thoughtfully put up the hood to shield his charge as far as possible from the curious gaze of the passersby. His charge was now chewing the pram cover and talking excitedly to itself. With a "heart steeled for any fate," William turned the corner into his own road. The baby's mother was standing at his gate.

"There you are!" she called. "I was getting quite anxious. Thank you *so* much, dear."

But that is what she said before she saw the baby!

CHAPTER 8

WILLIAM AND WHITE SATIN

"I'D simply love to have a page," murmured Miss Grant wistfully. "A wedding seems so—second-rate without a page."

Mrs. Brown, her aunt and hostess, looked across the tea-table at her younger son, who was devouring iced cake with that disregard for consequences which is the mark of youth.

"There's William," she said doubtfully. Then, "You've had quite enough cake, William."

Miss Grant studied William's countenance, which at that moment expressed intense virtue persecuted beyond all bearing.

"*Enough!*" he repeated. "I've had hardly any yet. I was only jus' beginning to have some when you looked at me. It's a plain cake. It won't do me any harm. I wu'nt eat it if it'd do me any harm. Sugar's *good* for you. Animals eat it to keep healthy. *Horses* eat it an' it don't do 'em any *harm*, an' polly parrots an' things eat it an' it don't—"

"Oh, don't argue, William," said his mother wearily.

William's gift of eloquence was known and feared in his family circle.

Then Miss Grant brought out the result of her study of his countenance.

"He's got such a—*modern* face!" she said. "There's something essentially medieval and romantic about the idea of a page."

Mrs. Brown (from whose house the wedding was to take place) looked worried.

"There's nothing medieval or romantic about William," she said.

"Well"—Miss Grant's face lit up—"what about his cousin Dorita. They're about the same age, aren't they? Both eleven. Well, the *two* of them in white satin with bunches of holly. Don't you think? Would you mind having her to stay for the ceremony?" (Miss Grant always referred to her wedding as "the ceremony.") "If you don't have his hair cut for a bit, he mightn't look so bad."

William had retired to the garden with his three bosom friends—Ginger, Henry and Douglas—where he was playing his latest game of mountaineering. A plank had been placed against the garden wall, and up this scrambled the three, roped together and wearing feathers in their caps. William was wearing an old golf cap of his mother's, and mentally pictured himself as an impressive and heroic figure. Before they reached the top they invariably lost their foothold, rolled down the plank and fell in a confused and bruised heap at the bottom. The bruises in no way detracted from the charm of the game. To William the fascination of any game consisted mainly in the danger to life and limb involved. The game had been suggested by an old alpenstock which had been thoughtlessly presented to William by a friend of Mr. Brown's. The paint of the staircase and upstairs corridor had been completely ruined before the family knew of the gift, and the alpenstock had been confiscated for a week, then restored on the condition that it was not to be brought into the house. The result was the game of mountaineering up the plank. They carried the alpenstock in turns, but William had two turns running to mark the fact that he was its proud possessor.

Mrs. Brown approached William on the subject of his prospective rôle of page with a certain apprehension. The normal attitude of William's family towards William was one of apprehension.

"Would you like to go to Cousin Sybil's wedding?" she said.

"No, I wu'nt," said William without hesitation.

"Wouldn't you like to go dressed up?" she suggested hopefully.

"Red Injun?" said William with a gleam of hope.

"Er—no, not exactly."

"Pirate?"

"Not quite."

"I'd go as a Red Injun, or I'd go as a Pirate," he said firmly, "but I wu'nt go as anything else."

"A page," said Miss Grant's clear, melodious voice, "is a medieval and romantic idea, William. There's the glamour of chivalry about it that should appeal strongly to a boy of your age."

William turned his inscrutable countenance upon her and gave her a cold glare.

They discussed his costume in private.

"I've got a pair of lovely white silk stockings," said his mother. "They'd do for tights, and Ethel has got a satin petticoat that's just beginning to go in one place. I should think we could make some sort of costume from that, don't you? We'll buy some more white satin and get some patterns."

"No, I won't wear Ethel's ole clothes," said William smouldering. "You all jus' want to make me look ridiclus. You don't care how ridiclus I look. I shall be ridiclus all the rest of my life goin' about in Ethel's ole clothes. I jus' won't do it. I jus' won't go to any ole weddin'. No, I *don't* want to see Cousin Sybil married, an' I jus' *won't* be made look ridiclus in Ethel's ole clothes."

They reasoned and coaxed and threatened, but in vain. Finally William yielded to parental authority and went about his world with an air of a martyr doomed to the stake. Even the game of mountaineering had lost its charm and the alpenstock lay neglected against the garden wall. The attitude of his select circle of friends was not encouraging.

"Yah! *Page!* Who's goin' to be a *page*? Oh, crumbs! A

107

page all dressed up in white. *Dear* little Willie. Won't he look swe-e-e-et?"

Life became very full. It was passed chiefly in the avenging of insults. William cherished a secret hope that the result of this would be to leave him disfigured for life and so unable to attend the wedding. However, except for a large lump on his forehead, he was none the worse. He eyed the lump thoughtfully in his looking-glass and decided that with a little encouragement it might render his public appearance in an affair of romance an impossibility. But the pain which resulted from one heroic effort at banging it against the wall caused him to abandon the plan.

Dorita arrived the next week, and with her her small brother Michael, aged three. Dorita was slim and graceful, with a pale little oval face and dark, curling hair.

Miss Grant received her on the doorstep.

"Well, my little maid of honour?" she said in her flute-like tones. "Welcome! We're going to be such friends—you and me and William—the bride" (she blushed and bridled becomingly) "and her little page and her little maid of honour. William's a boy, and he's just a *leetle* bit thought-less and doesn't realise the romance of it all. I'm sure you will. I see it in your dear little face. We'll have some lovely talks together." Her eyes fell upon Michael and narrowed suddenly. "He'd look sweet too, in white satin, wouldn't he?" turning to Mrs. Brown. "He could walk between them . . . We could buy some more white satin . . ."

When they had gone the maid of honour turned dark, long-lashed, demure eyes upon William.

"Soft mug, that," she said in clear, refined tones, nodding in the direction of the door through which the tall figure of Miss Grant had just disappeared.

William was vaguely cheered by her attitude.

"Are you keen on this piffling wedding affair?" she went on carelessly, " 'cause I jolly well tell you I'm not."

William felt that he had found a kindred spirit. He un-bent so far as to take her to the garden shed to show her a field-mouse he had caught and was keeping in a cardboard box.

"I'm teachin' it to dance," he confided, "an' it oughter fetch a jolly lot of money when it can dance proper. Dancin' mice do, you know. They show 'em on the stage, and people on the stage get pounds an' pounds every night, so I bet mice do too—at least the folks the mice belong to what dance on the stage. I'm teachin' it to dance by holdin' a biscuit over its head and movin' it about. It bit me twice yesterday." He proudly displayed his mutilated finger. "I only caught it yesterday. It oughter learn all right to-day," he added hopefully.

Her intense disappointment, when the only trace of the field-mouse that could be found was the cardboard box with a hole gnawed at one corner, drew William's heart to her still more.

He avoided Henry, Douglas and Ginger. Henry, Douglas and Ginger had sworn to be at the church door to watch William descend from the carriage in the glory of his white satin apparel, and William felt that their friendship could not stand the strain.

He sat with Dorita on the cold and perilous perch of the garden wall and discussed Cousin Sybil and the wedding. Dorita's language delighted and fascinated William.

"She's a soppy old luny," she would remark sweetly, shaking her dark curls. "The soppiest old luny you'd see in any old place on *this* old earth, you betcher life! She's made of sop. I wouldn't be found dead in a ditch with her—wouldn't touch her with the butt-end of a barge-pole. She's an assified ostrich, she is. Humph!"

"Those children are a *leetle* disappointing as regards character—to a child lover like myself," confided Miss Grant to her intellectual fiancé. "I've tried to sound their depths, but there are no depths to sound. There is none of the mystery, the glamour, the 'clouds of glory' about them. They are so—so material."

The day of the ordeal drew nearer and nearer, and

William's spirits sank lower and lower. His life seemed to stretch before him—youth, manhood and old age—dreary and desolate, filled only with humiliation and shame. His prestige and reputation would be blasted for ever. He would no longer be William—the Red Indian, the pirate, the dare-devil. He would simply be the Boy Who Went to a Wedding Dressed in White Satin. Evidently there would be a surging crowd of small boys at the church door. Every boy for miles round who knew William even by sight had volunteered the information that he would be there. William was to ride with Dorita and Michael in the bride's carriage. In imagination he had already descended from the carriage and heard the chorus of jeers. His cheeks grew hot at the thought. His life for years afterwards would consist solely in the avenging of insults. He followed the figure of the blushing bride-to-be with a baleful glare. In his worst moments he contemplated murder. The violence of his outburst when his mother mildly suggested a wedding present to the bride from her page and maid of honour horrified her.

"I'm bein' made look ridiclus all the rest of my life," he ended. "I'm not givin' her no present. I know what I'd *like* to give her," he added darkly.

"Yes, and I *do*, too."

Mrs. Brown forebore to question further.

The day of the wedding dawned coldly bright and sunny. William's expressions of agony and complaints of various startling symptoms of serious illnesses were ignored by his experienced family circle.

Michael was dressed first of the three in his minute white satin suit and sent down into the drawing-room to play quietly. Then an unwilling William was captured from the sanctuary of the garden shed and dragged pale and pro-testing to the slaughter.

"Yes, an' I'll *die* pretty soon, pro'bly," he said pathetically, "and then p'r'aps you'll be a bit sorry, an' I shan't care."

In Michael there survived two of the instincts of primitive

man, the instinct of foraging for food and that of concealing it from his enemies when found. Earlier in the day he had paid a visit to the kitchen and found it empty. Upon the table lay a pound of butter and a large bag of oranges. These he had promptly confiscated and, with a fear of interruption born of experience, he had retired with them under the table in the drawing-room. Before he could begin his feast he had been called upstairs to be dressed for the ceremony. On his return (immaculate in white satin) he found to his joy that his treasure trove had not been discovered. He began on the butter first. What he could not eat he smeared over his face and curly hair. Then he felt a sudden compunction and tried to remove all traces of the crime by rubbing his face and hair violently with a woolly mat. Then he sat down on the sofa and began the oranges. They were very yellow and juicy and rather overripe. He crammed them into his mouth with both little fat hands at once. He was well aware, even at his tender years, that life's sweetest joys come soonest to an end. Orange juice mingled with wool fluff and butter on his small round face. It trickled down his cheeks and fell on to his white lace collar. His mouth and the region round it were completely yellow. He had emptied the oranges out of the bag all around him on the seat. He was sitting in a pool of juice. His suit was covered with it, mingled with pips and skin, and still he ate on.

His first interruption was from William and Dorita, who came slowly downstairs holding hands in silent sympathy, two gleaming figures in white satin. They walked to the end of the room. They also had been sent to the drawing-room with orders to "play quietly" until summoned.

"*Play?*" William had echoed coldly. "I don't feel much like *playing*."

They stared at Michael, open-mouthed and speechless. Lumps of butter and bits of wool stuck in his curls and adhered to the upper portion of his face. They had been washed away from the lower portion of it by orange juice.

His suit was almost covered with it. Behind he was saturated with it.

"*Crumbs!*" said William at last.

"*You'll* catch it," remarked his sister.

Michael retreated hastily from the scene of his misdeeds. "Mickyth good now," he lisped deprecatingly.

They looked at the seat he had left—a pool of crushed orange fragments and juice. Then they looked at each other.

"*He'll* not be able to go," said Dorita slowly.

Again they looked at the empty orange-covered sofa and again they looked at each other.

"Heth kite good now," said Michael hopefully.

Then the maid of honour, aware that cold deliberation often kills the most glorious impulses, seized William's hand.

"Sit down. *Quick!*" she whispered sharply.

Without a word they sat down. They sat till they felt the cold moisture penetrate to their skins. Then William heaved a deep sigh.

"*We* can't go now," he said.

Through the open door they saw a little group coming— Miss Grant in shining white, followed by William's mother, arrayed in her brightest and best, and William's father, whose expression revealed a certain weariness mingled with a relief that the whole thing would soon be over.

"Here's the old sardine all togged up," whispered Dorita.

"William! Dorita! Michael!" they called.

Slowly William, Dorita and Michael obeyed the summons.

When Miss Grant's eyes fell upon the strange object that was Michael, she gave a loud scream.

"*Michael!* Oh, the *dreadful* child!"

She clasped the centre of the door and looked as though about to swoon.

Michael began to sob.

"*Poor* Mickey," he said through his tears. "He feelth tho thick."

They removed him hastily.

"Never mind, dear," said Mrs. Brown soothingly, "the other two look sweet."

But Mr. Brown had wandered farther into the room and thus obtained a sudden and startling view of the page and maid of honour from behind.

"What? Where?" he began explosively.

William and Dorita turned to him instinctively, thus providing Mrs. Brown and the bride with the spectacle that had so disturbed him.

The bride gave a second scream—shriller and wilder than the first.

"Oh, what have they done? Oh, the *wretched* children! And just when I wanted to feel *calm*. Just when all depends on my feeling *calm*. Just when—"

"We was walkin' round the room an' we sat down on the sofa and there was this stuff on it an' it came on our clothes," explained William stonily and monotonously and all in one breath.

"*Why* did you sit down?" said his mother.

"We was walkin' round an' we jus' felt tired and we sat down on the sofa and there was this stuff on it an' it came on—"

"Oh, *stop*! Didn't you *see* it there?"

William considered.

"Well, we was jus' walking round the room," he said, "an' we jus' felt tired and we sat—"

"*Stop* saying that."

"Couldn't we make *cloaks*?" wailed the bride, "to hang down and cover them all up behind. It wouldn't take long—"

Mr. Brown took out his watch.

"The carriage has been waiting a quarter of an hour already," he said firmly. "We've no time to spare. Come along, my dear. We'll continue the investigation after the service. You can't go, of course, you must stay at home now," he ended, turning a stern eye upon William. There was an unconscious note of envy in his voice.

"And I did so *want* to have a page," said Miss Grant plaintively as she turned away.

Joy and hope returned to William with a bound. As the sound of wheels was heard down the drive he turned head over heels several times on the lawn, then caught sight of his long-neglected alpenstock leaning against a wall.

"Come on," he shouted joyfully. "I'll teach you a game I made up. It's mountaineerin'."

She watched him place a plank against the wall and begin his perilous ascent.

"You're a mug," she said in her clear, sweet voice. "I know a mountaineering game worth ten of that old thing."

And it says much for the character and moral force of the maid of honour that William meekly put himself in the position of pupil.

It must be explained at this point that the domestics of the Brown household were busy arranging refreshments in a marquee in the garden. The front hall was quite empty.

In about a quarter of an hour the game of mountaineering was in full swing. On the lowest steps of the staircase reposed the mattress from William's father's and mother's bed, above it the mattress from Miss Grant's bed, above that the mattress from William's bed, and on the top, the mattress from Dorita's bed. In all the bedrooms the bed-clothes lay in disarray on the floor. A few nails driven through the ends of the mattresses into the stairs secured the stability of the "mountain." Still wearing their robes of ceremony, they scrambled up in stockinged feet, every now and then losing foothold and rolling down to the pile of pillows and bolsters (taken indiscriminately from all the beds) which was arranged at the foot of the staircase. Their mirth was riotous and uproarious. They used the alpenstock in turns. It was a great help. They could get a firm hold on the mattresses with the point of the alpenstock. William stood at the top of the mountain, hot and panting, his alpenstock in his hand, and paused for breath. He was well aware that retribution was not far off—was in the neighbouring church, to be quite exact, and would return in a carriage within the next few minutes. He was aware that an explanation of the yellow stain was yet to be demanded. He was aware that this was not a use to which the family mattresses could legitimately be put. But he cared for none of these things. In his mind's eye he only saw a crowd of small boys assembled outside a church door with eager eyes fixed on a carriage from which descended— Miss Grant, Mrs. Brown and Mr. Brown. His life stretched before him bright and rose-coloured. A smile of triumph curved his lips.

"Yah! Who waited at a church for someone what never came? Yah!"

"I hope you didn't get a bad cold waitin' for me on Wednesday at the church door."

"Some folks is easy had. I bet you all believed I was coming on Wednesday."

Such sentences floated idly through his mind.

"I say, my turn for that stick with the spike."

William handed it to her in silence.

"I say," she repeated, "what do you think of this marriage business?"

"Dunno," said William laconically.

"If I'd got to marry," went on the maid of honour, "I'd as soon marry *you* as anyone."

"I wu'nt mind," said the page gallantly. "But," he added hastily, "in ornery clothes."

"Oh, yes," she lost her foothold and rolled down to the pile of pillows. From them came her voice muffled, but clear as ever. "You betcher life. In ornery clothes."

CHAPTER 9

WILLIAM'S NEW YEAR'S DAY

WILLIAM went whistling down the street, his hands in his pockets. William's whistle was more penetrating than melodious. Sensitive people fled shuddering at the sound. The proprietor of the sweet shop, however, was not sensitive. He nodded affably as William passed. William was a regular customer of his—as regular, that is, as a wholly inadequate allowance would permit. Encouraged, William paused at the doorway and ceased to whistle.

" 'Ullo, Mr. Moss!" he said.

" 'Ullo, William!" said Mr. Moss.

"Anythin' cheap to-day?" went on William hopefully. Mr. Moss shook his head.

"Twopence a quarter cheapest," he said.

William sighed.

"That's awful *dear*," he said.

"What isn't dear? Tell me that. What isn't dear?" said Mr. Moss lugubriously.

"Well, gimme two ounces. I'll pay you to-morrow," said William casually.

Mr. Moss shook his head.

"Go on!" said William. "I get my money to-morrow. You know I get my money to-morrow."

"Cash, young sir," said Mr. Moss heavily. "My terms is cash. 'Owever," he relented, "I'll give you a few over when the scales is down to-morrow for a New Year's gift."

"Honest Injun?"

"Honest Injun."

"Well, gimme them now then," said William.

Mr. Moss hesitated.

"They wouldn't be no New Year's gift then, would they?" he said.

William considered.

"I'll eat 'em to-day but I'll *think* about 'em to-morrow," he promised. "That'll make 'em a New Year's gift."

Mr. Moss took out a handful of assorted fruit drops and passed them to William. William received them gratefully.

"An' what good resolution are you going to make to-morrow?" went on Mr. Moss.

William crunched in silence for a minute, then,

"Good resolution?" he questioned. "I ain't got none."

"You've got to have a good resolution for New Year's Day," said Mr. Moss firmly.

"Same as giving up sugar in tea at Lent and wearing blue on Oxford and Cambridge Boat Race Day?" said William with interest.

"Yes, same as that. Well, you've got to think of some fault you'd like to cure and start to-morrow."

William pondered.

"Can't think of anything," he said at last. "You think of something for me."

"You might make one to do your school work properly," he suggested.

William shook his head.

"No," he said, "that wun't be much fun, would it? Crumbs! It *wun't!*"

"Or—to keep your clothes tidy?" went on his friend.

William shuddered at the thought.

"Or to—give up shouting and whistling."

William crammed two more sweets into his mouth and shook his head very firmly.

"Crumbs, no!" he ejaculated indistinctly.

"Or to be polite."

"Perlite?"

"Yes. 'Please' and 'thank you,' and 'if you don't mind me sayin' so,' and 'if you excuse me contradictin' of you," and 'can I do anything for you?' and such like."

William was struck with this.

"Yes, I might be that," he said. He straightened his collar and stood up. "Yes, I might try bein' that. How long has it to go on, though?"

"Not long," said Mr. Moss. "Only the first day gen'rally. Folks gen'rally give 'em up after that."

"What's yours?" said William, putting four sweets into his mouth as he spoke.

Mr. Moss looked round his little shop with the air of a conspirator, then leant forward confidentially.

"I'm goin' to arsk 'er again," he said.

"Who?" said William, mystified.

"Someone I've arsked reg'lar every New Year's Day for ten year."

"Asked what?" said William, gazing at his last sweet.

"Arsked to take me, o' course," said Mr. Moss with an air of contempt for William's want of intelligence.

"Take you where?" said William. "Where d'you want to go? Why can't you go yourself?"

"Ter *marry* me, I means," said Mr. Moss, blushing slightly as he spoke.

"Well," said William with a judicial air, "I wun't have asked the same one for ten years. I'd have tried someone else. I'd have gone on asking other people, if I wanted to get married. You'd be sure to find someone that wouldn't mind you—with a sweet shop, too. She must be a softie. Does she *know* you've got a sweet shop?"

Mr. Moss merely sighed and popped a bull's eye into his mouth with an air of abstracted melancholy.

The next morning William leapt out of bed with an expression of stern resolve. "I'm goin' to be p'lite," he remarked to his bedroom furniture. "I'm goin' to be p'lite all day."

He met his father on the stairs as he went down to breakfast.

"Good mornin', Father," he said, with what he fondly imagined to be a courtly manner. "Can I do anything for you to-day?"

His father looked down at him suspiciously.

"What do you want now?" he demanded.

William was hurt.

"I'm only bein' p'lite. It's—you know—one of those things you make on New Year's Day. Well, I've made one to be p'lite."

His father apologised. "I'm sorry," he said. "You see, I'm not used to it. It startled me."

At breakfast William's politeness shone forth in all its glory.

"Can I pass you anything, Robert?" he said sweetly.

His elder brother coldly ignored him. "Going to rain again," he said to the world in general.

"If you'll 'scuse me contradicting of you, Robert," said William, "I heard the milkman sayin' it was goin' to be fine. If you'll 'scuse me contradictin' you."

"Look here!" said Robert angrily. "Less of your cheek!"

"Seems to me no one in this house understands wot bein' p'lite is," said William bitterly. "Seems to me one might go on bein' p'lite in this house for years an' no one would know wot one was doin'."

His mother looked at him anxiously.

"You're feeling quite well, dear, aren't you?" she said. "You haven't got a headache or anything, have you?"

"No. I'm bein' *p'lite*," he said irritably, then pulled himself up suddenly. "I'm quite well, thank you, Mother dear," he said in a tone of cloying sweetness.

"Does it hurt you very much?" inquired his brother tenderly.

"No, thank you, Robert," said William politely.

After breakfast he received his pocket-money with courteous gratitude.

"Thank you very much, Father."

"Not at all. Pray don't mention it, William. It's quite all

right," said Mr. Brown, not to be outdone. Then, "It's rather trying. How long does it last?"

"What?"

"The resolution."

"Oh, bein' p'lite! He said they didn't often do it after the first day."

"He's quite right, whoever he is," said Mr. Brown. "They don't."

"He's goin' to ask her again," volunteered William.

"Who ask who what?" said Mr. Brown, but William had departed. He was already on his way to Mr. Moss's shop.

Mr. Moss was at the door, hatted and coated, and gazing anxiously down the street.

"Goo' mornin', Mr. Moss," said William politely.

Mr. Moss took out a large antique watch.

"He's late!" he said. "I shall miss the train. Oh, dear! It will be the first New Year's Day I've missed in ten years."

William was inspecting the sweets with the air of an expert.

"Them pink ones are new," he said at last. "How much are they?"

"Eightpence a quarter. Oh, dear, I shall miss the train."

"They're very small ones," said William disparagingly. "You'd think they'd be less than that—small ones like that."

"Will you—will you do something for me and I'll *give* you a quarter of those sweets?"

William gasped. The offer was almost too munificent to be true.

"I'll do *anythin'* for that," he said simply.

"Well, just stay in the shop till my nephew Bill comes. 'E'll be 'ere in two shakes an' I'll miss my train if I don't go now. 'E's goin' to keep the shop for me till I'm back an' 'e'll be 'ere any minute now. Jus' tell 'im I 'ad to run for to catch my train an' if anyone comes into the shop before 'e comes jus' tell 'em to wait or to come back later. You can weigh yourself a quarter o' those sweets."

Mr. Moss was certainly in a holiday mood. William pinched himself to just make sure that he was still alive and had not been translated suddenly to the realms of the blessed.

Mr. Moss, with a last anxious glance at his watch, hurried off in the direction of the station.

William was left alone. He spent a few moments indulging in roseate daydreams. The ideal of his childhood—perhaps of everyone's childhood—was realised. He had a sweet shop. He walked round the shop with a conscious swagger, pausing to pop into his mouth a Butter Ball—composed, as the label stated, of pure farm cream and best butter. It was all his—all those rows and rows of gleaming bottles of sweets of every size and colour, those boxes and boxes of attractively arranged chocolates. Deliberately he imagined himself as their owner. By the time he had walked round the shop three times he believed that he was the owner.

At this point a small boy appeared in the doorway. William scowled at him.

"Well," he said ungraciously, "what d'you want?" Then, suddenly remembering his resolution, "*Please*, what d'you want?"

"Where's Uncle?" said the small boy with equal ungraciousness. " 'Cause our Bill's ill an' can't come."

William waved him off.

"That's all right," he said. "You tell 'em that's all right. That's quite all right. See? Now, you go off!"

The small boy stood as though rooted to the spot. William pressed into one of his hands a stick of licorice and into the other a packet of chocolate.

"Now, you go *away*! I don't *want* you here. See? You go *away* you little—bird-brained bluebottle!"

William's invective was often wholly original.

The small boy made off, still staring and clutching his spoils. William started to the door and yelled to the retreating figure, "If you don't mind me sayin' so."

He had already come to look upon the Resolution as a kind of god who must at all costs be propitiated. Already the Resolution seemed to have bestowed upon him the dream of his life—a fully-equipped sweet shop.

He wandered round again and discovered a wholly new sweetmeat called Cokernut Kisses. Its only drawback was its instability. It melted away in the mouth at once. So much so that almost before William was aware of it he was confronted by the empty box. He returned to the more solid charms of the Pineapple Crisp.

He was interrupted by the entrance of a thin lady of uncertain age.

"Good morning," she said icily. "Where's Mr. Moss?"

William answered as well as the presence of five sweets in his mouth would allow him.

"I can't hear a word you say," she said—more frigidly than ever.

William removed two of his five sweets and placed them temporarily on the scale.

"Gone," he said laconically, then murmured vaguely, "thank you," as the thought of the Resolution loomed up in his mind.

"Who's in charge?"

"Me," said William ungrammatically.

She looked at him with distinct disapproval.

"Well, I'll have one of those bars of chocolate."

William, looking round the shop, realised suddenly that his own depredations had been on no small scale. But there was a chance of making good any loss that Mr. Moss might otherwise have sustained.

He looked down at the twopenny bars.

"Shillin' each," he said firmly.

She gasped.

"They were only twopence yesterday."

"They're gone up since," said William brazenly, adding a vague, "if you'll kin'ly 'scuse me sayin' so."

"Gone up——?" she repeated indignantly. "Have you heard from the makers they've gone up?"

"Yes'm," said William politely.

"When did you hear?"

"This mornin'—if you don't mind me saying so."

William's manner of fulsome politeness seemed to madden her.

"Did you hear by post?"

"Yes'm. By post this mornin'."

She glared at him with vindictive triumph.

"I happen to live opposite, you wicked, lying boy, and I know that the postman did not call here this morning."

William met her eye calmly.

"No, they came round to see me in the night—the makers did. You cou'n't of heard them," he added hastily. "It was when you was asleep. If you'll 'scuse me contradictin' of you."

It is a great gift to be able to lie so as to convince other people. It is still a greater gift to be able to lie so as to convince oneself. William was possessed of the latter gift.

"I shall certainly not pay more than twopence," said his customer severely, taking a bar of chocolate and laying down twopence on the counter. "And I shall report this shop to the Profiteering Committee. It's scandalous. And a pack of wicked lies!"

William scowled at her.

"They're a *shillin'*," he said. "I don't want your nasty ole tuppences. I said they was a *shillin'*."

He followed her to the door. She was crossing the street to her house. "You—you ole *thief*!" he yelled after her, though, true to his Resolution, he added softly with dogged determination, "if you don't mind me sayin' so."

"I'll set the police on you," his late customer shouted angrily back across the street. "You wicked, blasphemous boy!"

William put out his tongue at her, then returned to the shop and closed the door.

Here he discovered that the door, when opened, rang a bell, and, after filling his mouth with Liquorice All Sorts, he spent the next five minutes vigorously opening and shutting the door till something went wrong with the mechanism of the bell. At this he fortified himself with a course of Nutty Footballs and, standing on a chair, began ruthlessly to dismember the bell. He was disturbed by the entry of another customer. Swallowing a Nutty Football whole, he hastened to his post behind the counter.

The newcomer was a little girl of about nine—a very dainty little girl, dressed in a white fur coat and hat. Her hair fell in golden curls over her white fur shoulders. Her eyes were blue. Her cheeks were velvety and rosy. Her mouth was like a baby's. William had seen this vision on various occasions in the town, but had never yet addressed it. Whenever he had seen it, his heart in the midst of his body had been even as melting wax. He smiled—a self-conscious, sheepish smile. His freckled face blushed to the roots of his short stubby hair. She seemed to find nothing odd in the fact of a small boy being in charge of a sweet shop. She came up to the counter.

"Please, I want two twopenny bars of chocolate."

Her voice was very clear and silvery.

Ecstasy rendered William speechless. His smile grew wider and more foolish. Seeing his two half-sucked Pineapple Crisps exposed upon the scales, he hastily put them into his mouth.

She laid four pennies on the counter.

William found his voice.

"You can have lots for that," he said huskily. "They've gone cheap. They've gone ever so cheap. You can take all the boxful for that," he went on recklessly. He pressed the box into her reluctant hands. "An'—what else would you like? You jus' tell me that. Tell me what else you'd like?"

"Please, I haven't any more money," gasped a small bewildered voice.

"*Money* don't matter," said William. "Things is cheap

124

to-day. Things is awful cheap to-day. *Awful* cheap! You can have—anythin' you like for that fourpence. Anythin' you like."

" 'Cause it's New Year's Day?" said the vision, with a gleam of understanding.

"Yes," said William, " 'cause it's that."

"Is it your shop?"

"Yes," said William, with an air of importance. "It's all my shop."

She gazed at him in admiration and envy.

"I'd love to have a sweet shop," she said wistfully.

"Well, you take anythin' you like," said William generously.

She collected as much as she could carry and started towards the door. "*Sank* you! Sank you ever so!" she said gratefully.

William stood leaning against the door in the easy attitude of the good-natured, all-providing male.

"It's all right," he said with an indulgent smile. "Quite all right. Quite all right." Then, with an inspiration born of memories of his father earlier in the day: "Not at all. Don't menshun it. Not at all. Quite all right."

He stopped, simply for lack of further expressions, and bowed with would-be gracefulness as she went through the doorway.

As she passed the window she was rewarded by a spreading effusive smile in a flushed face.

She stopped and kissed her hand.

William blinked with pure emotion.

He continued his smile long after its recipient had disappeared. Then absent-mindedly he crammed his mouth with a handful of Mixed Dew Drops and sat down behind the counter.

As he crunched Mixed Dew Drops he indulged in a daydream in which he rescued the little girl in the white fur coat from robbers and pirates and a burning house. He was just leaping nimbly from the roof of the burning house, holding the little girl in the white fur coat in his arms, when he caught sight of two of his friends flattening their noses at the window. He rose from his seat and went to the door.

" 'Ullo, Ginger! 'Ullo, Henry!" he said with an unsuccessful effort to appear void of self-consciousness.

They gazed at him in wonder.

"I've gotta shop," he went on casually. "Come on in an' look at it."

They peeped round the doorway cautiously and, reassured by the sight of William obviously in sole possession, they entered, open-mouthed. They gazed at the boxes and bottles of sweets. Aladdin's Cave was nothing to this.

"How'd you get it, William?" gasped Ginger.

"Someone gave it me," said William. "I made one of them things to be p'lite an' someone gave it me. Go on," he said kindly. "Jus' help yourselves. Not at all. Jus' help yourselves an' don't menshun it."

They needed no second bidding. With the unerring instinct of childhood (not unsupported by experience) that at any minute their Eden might be invaded by the avenging angel in the shape of a grown-up, they made full use of their time. They went from box to box, putting handfuls of sweets and chocolates into their mouths. They said nothing, simply because speech was, under the circumstances, a physical impossibility. Showing a foresight for the future, worthy of the noble ant itself, so often held up as a model to childhood, they filled pockets in the intervals of cramming their mouths.

A close observer might have noticed that William now ate little. William himself had been conscious for some time of a curious and inexplicable feeling of coldness towards the tempting dainties around him. He was, however, loath to give in to the weakness, and every now and then he nonchalantly put into his mouth a Toasted Square or a Fruity Bit.

It happened that a loutish boy of about fourteen was passing the shop. At the sight of three small boys rapidly consuming the contents, he became interested.

"What yer doin' of?" he said indignantly, standing in the doorway.

"You get out of my shop," said William valiantly.

"*Yer* shop?" said the boy. "Yer bloomin' well pinchin' things out o' someone else's shop, *I* can see. 'Ere, gimme some of them."

"You get *out*!" said William.

"Get out *yerself*!" said the other.

"If I'd not made one to be p'lite," said William threateningly, "I'd knock you down."

"Yer would, would yer?" said the other, beginning to roll up his sleeves.

"Yes, an' I would too. You get out." Seizing the nearest bottle, which happened to contain Acid Drops, he began to fire them at his opponent's head. One hit him in the eye. He retired into the street. William, now aflame for battle, followed him, still hurling Acid Drops with all his might. A crowd of boys collected together. Some gathered Acid Drops from the gutter, others joined the scrimmage. William, Henry and Ginger carried on a noble fight against heavy odds.

It was only the sight of the proprietor of the shop coming briskly down the side-walk that put an end to the battle. The street boys made off (with what spoils they could gather) in one direction, and Ginger and Henry in another. William, clasping an empty Acid Drop bottle to his bosom, was left to face Mr. Moss.

Mr. Moss entered and looked round with an air of bewilderment.

"Where's Bill?" he said.

"He's ill," said William. "He couldn't come. I've been keepin' shop for you. I've done the best I could." He looked round the rifled shop and hastened to propitiate the owner as far as possible. "I've got some money for you," he added soothingly, pointing to the six pennies that represented his morning's takings. "It's not much," he went on with some truth, looking again at the rows of emptied boxes and half-emptied bottles and the debris that is always and everywhere the inevitable result of a battle. But Mr. Moss hardly seemed to notice it.

"Thanks, William," he said almost humbly. "William, she's took me. She's goin' ter marry me. Isn't it grand? After all these years!"

"I'm afraid there's a bit of a mess," said William, returning to the more important matter.

Mr. Moss waved aside his apologies.

"It doesn't matter, William," he said. "Nothing matters to-day. She's took me at last. I'm goin' to shut shop this afternoon and go over to her again. Thanks for staying, William."

"Not at all. Don't menshun it," said William nobly. Then, "I think I've had enough of that bein' p'lite. Will one mornin' do for this year, d'you think?"

"Er—yes. Well, I'll shut up. Don't you stay, William. You'll want to be getting home for lunch."

Lunch? Quite definitely William decided that he did not want any lunch. The very thought of lunch brought with it a feeling of active physical discomfort which was much more than mere absence of hunger. He decided to go home as quickly as possible, though not to lunch.

"Goo'-bye," he said.

"Good-bye," said Mr. Moss.

"I'm afraid you'll find some things gone," said William faintly; "some boys was in."

"That's all right, William," said Mr. Moss, roused again from his rosy dreams. "That's quite all right."

But it was not "quite all right" with William. Reader, if you had been left, at the age of eleven, in sole charge of a sweet shop for a whole morning, would it have been "all right" with you? I trow not. But we will not follow William through the humiliating hours of the afternoon. We will leave him as, pale and unsteady, but as yet master of the situation, he wends his homeward way.

CHAPTER 10

"JUMBLE"

WILLIAM'S father carefully placed the bow and arrows at the back of the cupboard, then closed the cupboard door and locked it in grim silence. William's eyes, large, reproachful, and gloomy, followed every movement.

"Three windows and Mrs. Clive's cat all in one morning," began Mr. Brown sternly.

"I didn't *mean* to hit that cat," said William earnestly. "I didn't—honest. I wouldn't go round teasin' cats. They get so mad at you, cats do. It jus' got in the way. I couldn't stop shootin' in time. An' I didn't *mean* to break those windows. I wasn't *tryin'* to hit them. I've not hit anything I was trying to hit yet," wistfully. "I've not got into it. It's jus' a knack. It jus' wants practice."

Mr. Brown pocketed the key.

"It's a knack you aren't likely to acquire by practice on this instrument," he said drily.

William wandered out into the garden and looked sadly up at the garden wall. But The Little Girl Next Door was away and could offer no sympathy, even if he climbed up to his precarious seat on the top. Fate was against him in every way. With a deep sigh he went out of the garden gate and strolled down the road disconsolately, hands in pockets.

Life stretched empty and uninviting before him without his bow and arrows. And Ginger would have his bow and arrows, Henry would have his bow and arrows, Douglas would have his bow and arrows. He, William, alone would be a thing apart, a social outcast, a boy without a bow and arrows; for bows and arrows were the fashion. If only one

E

of the others would break a window or hit a silly old cat that hadn't the sense to keep out of the way.

He came to a stile leading into a field and took his seat upon it dejectedly, his elbows on his knees, his chin in his hands. Life was simply not worth living.

"A rotten old cat!" he said aloud, "a rotten old cat!— and didn't even hurt it. It—it made a fuss—jus' out of spite, screamin' and carryin' on! And windows!—as if glass wasn't cheap enough—and easy to put in. I could—I could mend 'em myself—if I'd got the stuff to do it. I—" He stopped. Something was coming down the road. It came jauntily with a light, dancing step, fox-terrier ears cocked, retriever nose raised, collie tail wagging, slightly dachshund body a-quiver with the joy of life.

It stopped in front of William with a glad bark of welcome, then stood eager, alert, friendly, a mongrel unashamed.

"Rats! Fetch 'em out!" said William idly.

It gave a little spring, and waited, front paws apart and crouching, a waggish eye upraised to William. William broke off a stick from the hedge and threw it. His visitor darted after it with a shrill bark, took it up, worried it, threw it into the air, caught it, growled at it, finally brought it back to William, and waited, panting, eager, unmistakably grinning, begging for more.

William's drooping spirits revived. He descended from his perch and examined its collar. It bore the one word, "Jumble."

"Hey! Jumble!" he called, setting off down the road.

Jumble jumped up and around him, dashed off, dashed back, worried his boots, jumped up at him again in wild, eager friendship, dashed off again, begged for another stick, caught it, rolled over with it, growled at it, then chewed it up and laid the remains at William's feet.

"Good ole chap!" said William encouragingly. "Good ole Jumble! Come on, then."

Jumble came on. William walked through the village

with a self-conscious air of proud yet careless ownership, while Jumble gambolled round his heels.

Every now and then he would turn his head and whistle imperiously, to recall his straying protégé from the investigation of ditches and roadside. It was a whistle, commanding, controlling, yet withal careless, that William had sometimes practised privately in readiness for the blissful day when Fate should present him with a real live dog of his own. So far Fate, in the persons of his father and mother, had been proof against all his pleading.

William passed a blissful morning. Jumble swam in the pond, he fetched sticks out of it, he shook himself violently all over William, he ran after a hen, he was chased by a cat, he barked at a herd of cows, he pulled down a curtain that was hanging out in a cottage garden to dry—he was mischievous, affectionate, humorous, utterly irresistible—and he completely adopted William. William would turn a corner with a careless swagger and then watch breathlessly to see if the rollicking, frisky little figure would follow, and always it came tearing eagerly after him.

William was rather late for lunch. His father and mother and elder brother and sister were just beginning the meal. He slipped quietly and unostentatiously into his seat. His father was reading a newspaper. Mr. Brown always took two daily papers, one of which he perused at breakfast and the other at lunch.

"William," said Mrs. Brown, "I do wish you'd be in time, and I do wish you'd brush your hair before you come to table."

William raised a hand to perform the operation, but catching sight of its colour, hastily lowered it.

"No, Ethel dear, I didn't know anyone had taken Lavender Cottage. An artist? How nice! William, dear, *do* sit still. Have they moved in yet?"

"Yes," said Ethel, "they've taken it furnished for two months, I think. Oh, my goodness, just *look* at William's hands!"

William put his hands under the table and glared at her.

"Go and wash your hands, dear," said Mrs. Brown patiently.

For eleven years she had filled the trying position of William's mother. It had taught her patience.

William rose reluctantly.

"They're not dirty," he said in a tone of righteous indignation. "Well, anyway, they've been dirtier other times and you've said nothin'. I can't be *always* washin' them, can I? Some sorts of hands get dirty quicker than others an' if you keep on washin' it only makes them worse an'—"

Ethel groaned and William's father lowered his paper. William withdrew quickly but with an air of dignity.

"And just *look* at his shoes!" said Ethel as he went. "Simply caked; and his socks are soaking wet—you can see from here. He's been right *in* the pond by the look of him, and—"

William heard no more. There were moments when he actively disliked Ethel.

He returned a few minutes later, shining with cleanliness, his hair brushed back fiercely off his face.

"His *nails*," murmured Ethel as he sat down.

"Well," said Mrs. Brown, "go on telling us about the new people. William, do hold your knife properly, dear. Yes, Ethel?"

William finished his meal in silence, then brought forth his momentous announcement.

"I've gotter dog," he said with an air of importance.

"What sort of a dog?" and "Who gave it to you?" said Robert and Ethel simultaneously.

"No one gave it me," he said. "I jus' got it. It began following me this morning an' I couldn't get rid of it. It wouldn't go, anyway. It followed me all round the village an' it came home with me. I couldn't get rid of it, anyhow."

"Where is it now?" said Mr. Brown anxiously.

"In the back garden."

Mr. Brown folded up his paper.

"Digging up my flower-beds, I suppose," he said with despairing resignation.

"He's tied up all right," William reassured him. "I tied him to the tree in the middle of the rose-bed."

"The rose-bed!" groaned his father. "Good Lord!"

"Has he had anything to eat?" demanded Robert sternly.

"Yes," said William, avoiding his mother's eye. "I found a few bits of old things for him in the larder."

William's father took out his watch and rose from the table.

"Well, you'd better take it to the police station this afternoon," he said shortly.

"The police station!" repeated William hoarsely. "It's not a *lost* dog. It—it jus' doesn't belong to anyone, at least it didn't. Poor thing," feelingly. "It—it doesn't want *much* to make it happy. It can sleep in my room an' jus' eat scraps."

"You'll have to take it, you know, William," said Mrs. Brown, "so be quick. You know where the police station is, don't you? Shall I come with you?"

"No, thank you," said William hastily.

A few minutes later he was walking down to the police station followed by the still eager Jumble, who trotted along, unconscious of his doom.

Upon William's face was a set, stern expression which cleared slightly as he neared the police station. He stood at the gate and looked at Jumble. Jumble placed his front paws ready for a game and wagged his tail.

"Well," said William, "here you are. Here's the police station."

Jumble gave a shrill bark. "Hurry up with that stick or that race, whichever you like," he seemed to say.

"Well, go in," said William, nodding his head in the direction of the door.

Jumble began to worry a big stone in the road. He rolled it along with his paws, then ran after it with fierce growls.

"Well, it's the police station," said William. "Go in if you want."

With that he turned on his heel and walked home, without one backward glance. But he walked slowly, with many encouraging "Hey! Jumbles" and many short commanding whistles. And Jumble trotted happily at his heels. There was no one in the garden, there was no one in the hall, there was no one on the stairs. Fate was for once on William's side.

William appeared at the tea-table well washed and brushed, wearing that air of ostentatious virtue that those who knew him best connected with his most daring coups.

"Did you take that dog to the police station, William?" said William's father.

William coughed.

"Yes, Father," he said meekly, with his eyes upon his plate.

"What did they say about it?"

"Nothing, Father."

"I suppose I'd better spend the evening replanting those rose-trees," went on his father bitterly.

"And William gave him a *whole* steak and kidney pie," murmured Mrs. Brown. "Cook will have to make another for to-morrow."

William coughed again politely but did not raise his eyes from his plate.

"What is that noise?" said Ethel. "Listen!"

They sat, listening intently. There was a dull grating sound as of the scratching of wood.

"It's upstairs," said Robert, with the air of a Sherlock Holmes.

Then came a shrill, impatient bark.

"It's a *dog*!" said the four of them simultaneously. "It's William's dog."

They all turned horrified eyes upon William, who coloured slightly but continued to eat a piece of cake with an unconvincing air of abstraction.

"I thought you said you'd taken that dog to the police station, William," said Mr. Brown sternly.

"I did," said William with decision. "I did take it to the police station an' I came home. I s'pose it must've got out an' come home an' gone up into my bedroom."

"Where did you leave it? In the police station?"

"No—at it—jus' at the gate."

Mr. Brown rose with an air of weariness.

"Robert," he said, "will you please see that that animal goes to the police station this evening?"

"Yes, Father," said Robert, with a vindictive glare at William.

William followed him upstairs.

"Beastly nuisance!" muttered Robert.

Jumble, who was chewing William's door, greeted them ecstatically.

"Look!" said William bitterly. "Look at how it knows one! Nice thing to send a dog that knows one like that to the police station! Mean sort of trick!"

Robert surveyed it coldly.

"Rotten little mongrel!" he said from the heights of superior knowledge.

"Mongrel!" said William indignantly. "There jus' isn't no mongrel about _him_. Look at him! An' he can learn tricks easy as easy. Look at him sit up and beg. I only taught him this afternoon."

He took a biscuit out of his pocket and held it up. Jumble rose unsteadily on to his hind legs and tumbled over backwards. He wagged his tail and grinned, intensely amused. Robert's expression of superiority relaxed.

"Do it again," he said. "Not so far back. Here! Give it me. Come on, come on, old chap! That's it! Now stay there! Stay there! Good dog! Got any more? Let's try him again."

During the next twenty minutes they taught him to sit up and almost taught him "Trust" and "Paid for." There was certainly a charm about Jumble. Even

Robert felt it. Then Ethel's voice came up the stairs.

"Robert! Sydney Bellew's come for you."

"Blow the wretched dog!" said the fickle Robert rising, red and dishevelled from stooping over Jumble. "We were going to walk to Fairfields and the beastly police station's right out of our way."

"I'll take it, Robert," said William kindly. "I will, really."

Robert eyed him suspiciously.

"Yes, you took it this afternoon, didn't you?"

"I will, honest, to-night, Robert. Well, I couldn't not, could I?—after all this."

"I don't know," said Robert darkly. "No one ever knows what *you* are going to do!"

Sydney's voice came up.

"Hurry up, old chap! We shall never have time to do it before dark, if you aren't quick."

"I'll take him, honest, Robert."

Robert hesitated and was lost.

"Well," he said, "you just mind you do, that's all, or I'll jolly well hear about it. I'll see *you* do, too."

So William started off once more towards the police station with Jumble, still blissfully happy, at his heels. William walked slowly, eyes fixed on the ground, brows knit in deep thought. It was very rarely that William admitted himself beaten.

"Hello, William!"

Ginger stood before him holding his bow and arrows ostentatiously.

"You've had your bow and arrows took off you!" he jeered.

William fixed his eye moodily upon him for a minute, then very gradually his eye brightened and his face cleared. William had an idea.

"If I give you a dog half time," he said slowly, "will you give me your bow and arrows half time?"

"Where's your dog?" said Ginger suspiciously.

William did not turn his head.

"There's one behind me, isn't there," he said anxiously. "Hey, Jumble!"

"Oh, yes, he's just come out of the ditch."

"Well," continued William, "I'm taking him to the police station and I'm just goin' on an' he's following me and if you take him off me I won't see you 'cause I won't turn round and jus' take hold of his collar an' he's called Jumble an' take him up to the old barn and we'll keep him there an' join at him and feed him days and days about and you let me practise on your bow and arrow. That's fair, isn't it?"

Ginger considered thoughtfully.

"All right," he said laconically.

William walked on to the police station without turning round.

"Well?" whispered Robert sternly that evening.

"I took him, Robert—least—I started off with him, but when I'd got there he'd gone. I looked round and he'd jus' gone. I couldn't see him anywhere, so I came home."

"Well, if he comes to this house again," said Robert, "I'll wring his neck, so just you look out."

Two days later William sat in the barn on an upturned box, chin in hands, gazing down at Jumble. A paper bag containing Jumble's ration for the day lay beside him. It was his day of ownership. The collecting of Jumble's "scraps" was a matter of infinite care and trouble. They consisted of—a piece of bread that William had managed to slip into his pocket during breakfast, a piece of meat he had managed to slip into his pocket during dinner, a jam puff stolen from the larder, and a bone removed from the dustbin. Ginger roamed the fields with his bow and arrows while William revelled in the ownership of Jumble. To-morrow William would roam the fields with bow and arrows and Ginger would assume ownership of Jumble.

William had spent the morning teaching Jumble several complicated tricks, and adoring him more and more completely each moment. He grudged him bitterly to Ginger, but—the charm of the bow and arrows was strong. He wished to terminate the partnership, to resign Ginger's bow and arrows and take the irresistible Jumble wholly to himself. He thought of the bow and arrows in the cupboard; he thought, planned, plotted, but could find no way out. He did not see a man come to the door of the barn and stand there leaning against the door-post watching him. He was a tall man with a thin, lean face and a loose-fitting tweed suit. As his eyes lit upon William and Jumble they narrowed suddenly and his mobile lips curved into a slight, unconscious smile. Jumble saw him first and went towards him wagging his tail. William looked up and scowled ungraciously. The stranger raised his hat.

"Good afternoon," he said politely. "Do you remember what you were thinking about just then?"

William looked at him with a certain interest, speculating upon his probable insanity. He imagined lunatics were amusing people.

"Yes."

"Well, if you'll think of it again and look just like that, I'll give you anything you like. It's a rash promise, but I will."

William promptly complied. He quite forgot the presence of the strange man, who took a little block out of his pocket and began to sketch William's inscrutable, brooding face.

"Daddy!"

The man sighed and put away his block.

"You'll do it again for me one day, won't you, and I'll keep my promise. Hello!"

A little girl appeared now at the barn door, dainty, dark-eyed and exquisitely dressed. She threw a lightning flash at the occupants of the barn.

"Daddy!" she screamed. "It's Jumble! It *is* Jumble! Oh, you horrid dog-stealing boy!"

Jumble ran to her with shrill barks of welcome, then ran back to William to reassure him of his undying loyalty.

"It *is* Jumble," said the man. "He's called Jumble," he explained to William, "because he is a jumble. He's all sorts of a dog, you know. This is Ninette, my daughter, and my name is Jarrow, and we've taken Lavender Cottage for two months. We're roving vagabonds. We never stay anywhere longer than two months. So now you know all about us. Jumble seems to have adopted you. Ninette, my dear, you are completely ousted from Jumble's heart. This gentleman reigns supreme."

"I *didn't* steal him," said William indignantly. "He just came. He began following me. I didn't want him to—not jus' at first anyway, not much, anyway. I suppose," a dreadful fear came to his heart, "I suppose you want him back?"

"You can keep him for a bit if you want him, can't he, Daddy? Daddy's going to buy me a Pom—a dear little white Pom. When we lost Jumble, I thought I'd rather have a Pom. Jumble's so rough and he's not really a *good* dog. I mean, he's no pedigree."

"Then can I keep him jus' for a bit?" said William, his voice husky with eagerness.

"Oh, yes. I'd much rather have a quieter sort of dog. Would you like to come and see our cottage? It's just over here."

William, slightly bewildered but greatly relieved, set off with her. Mr. Jarrow followed slowly behind. It appeared that Miss Ninette Jarrow was rather a wonderful person. She was eleven years old. She had visited every capital in Europe, seen the best art and heard the best music in each. She had been to every play then on in London. She knew all the newest dances.

"Do you like Paris?" she asked William as they went towards Lavender Cottage.

"Never been there," said William stolidly, glancing round surreptitiously to see that Jumble was following.

She shook her dark curly head from side to side—a little trick she had.

"You funny boy. *Mais vous parlez Français, n'est ce pas?*"

William disdained to answer. He whistled to Jumble, who was chasing an imaginary rabbit in a ditch.

She stopped suddenly under a tree and held up her little vivacious, piquant face to him.

"You can kiss me if you like," she said.

William looked at her dispassionately.

"I don't want to, thanks," he said politely.

"Oh, you *are* a funny boy!" she said with a ripple of laughter, "and you look so rough and untidy. You're rather like Jumble. Do you like Jumble?"

"Yes," said William. His voice had a sudden quaver in it. His ownership of Jumble was a thing of the past.

"You can have him for always and always," she said suddenly. "*Now* kiss me!"

He kissed her cheek awkwardly with the air of one determined to do his duty, but with a great, glad relief at his heart.

She raced back to her father with another ripple of laughter.

"He's *such* a funny boy, Daddy, I've given him Jumble and he didn't want to kiss me!"

Mr. Jarrow fixed William with a drily quizzical smile.

As they got to the door of Lavender Cottage he turned to William.

"Now just sit and think for a minute. I'll keep my promise."

"I do like you," said Ninette graciously as he took his departure. "You must come again. I think I'd like to marry you when we grow up. You're so—*restful.*"

William came home the next afternoon to find Mr. Jarrow in the arm-chair in the drawing-room talking to his father.

"I was just dry for a subject," he was saying; "at my wits' end, and when I saw him there, I had a Heaven-sent inspiration. Ah! here he is. Ninette wants you to come to tea to-morrow, William. Ninette's given him Jumble. Do you mind?" turning to Mr. Brown.

Mr. Brown swallowed hard.

"I'm trying not to," he said. "He kept us all awake last night, but I suppose we'll get used to it."

"And I made him a rash promise," went on Mr. Jarrow, "and I'm jolly well going to keep it if it's humanly possible. William, what would you like best in all the world?"

William fixed his eyes unflinchingly upon his father.

"I'd like my bow and arrows back out of that cupboard," he said firmly.

Mr. Jarrow looked at William's father beseechingly.

"Don't let me down," he implored. "I'll pay for all the damage."

Slowly and with a deep sigh, Mr. Brown drew a bunch of keys from his pocket.

"It means that we all go once more in hourly peril of our lives," he said resignedly.

After tea William set off again down the road. The setting sun had turned the sky to gold. There was a soft haze over all the countryside. The clear bird songs filled all the air, and the hedgerows were bursting into summer. And through it all marched William, with a slight swagger, his bow under one arm, his arrows under the other, while at his heels trotted Jumble, eager, playful, adoring—a mongrel unashamed—all sorts of a dog. And at William's heart was a proud, radiant happiness.

There was a picture in that year's Academy that attracted a good deal of attention. It was of a boy sitting on an up-turned box in a barn, his elbows on his knees, his chin in his hands. He was gazing down at a mongrel dog and in his freckled face was the solemnity and unconscious, eager wistfulness that is the mark of youth. His untidy, unbrushed hair stood up round his face. The mongrel was looking up, quivering, expectant, trusting, adoring, some reflection of the boy's eager wistfulness showing in the eyes and cocked ear. It was called "Friendship."

Mrs. Brown went up to see it. She said it wasn't really a

very good likeness of William and she wished they'd made him look a little tidier.

CHAPTER II

THE BEST LAID PLANS

"SHE'S—she's a real Botticelli," said the young man dreamily, as he watched the figure of William's sister, Ethel, disappearing into the distance.

William glared at him.

"Bottled cherry yourself!" he said indignantly. "She can't help havin' red hair, can she? No more'n you can help havin'—havin'—" his eye wandered speculatively over the young man in search of physical defects—"having big ears," he ended.

The young man did not resent the insult. He did not even hear it. His eyes were still fixed upon the slim figure in the distance.

" 'Eyes of blue and hair red-gold,' " he said softly. "Red-gold. I had to put that because it's got both colours in it. Red-gold, 'Eyes of blue and hair red-gold.' What rhymes with gold?"

"Cold," suggested William brightly. "That's jolly good too, 'cause she has gotter cold. She was sneezing all last night."

"No. It should be something about her heart being cold.

> *"Eyes of blue and hair red-gold,*
> *Heart of ice—so stony cold—"*

"That's jolly good!" said William with admiration. "It's just like what you read in real books—poetry books!"

The young man—James French by name—had met Ethel at a party and had succumbed to her charm. Lacking courage to pursue the acquaintance, he had cultivated the friendship of her small brother, under a quite erroneous impression that this would win him her good graces.

"What would you like most in the world?" he said suddenly, leaning forward from his seat on the top of the gate. "Suppose someone let you choose."

"White rats," said William without a moment's hesitation.

The young man was plunged in deep thought.

"I'm thinking of a way," he said at last. "I've nearly got it. Just walk home with me, will you? I'll give you something when we get there," he bribed with pathetic pleading, noting William's reluctant face. "I want to tell you my idea."

They walked down the lane together. The young man talked volubly and earnestly. William's mouth opened wide with amazement and disapproving horror. The words "white rats" were repeated frequently. Finally William nodded his head, as though acquiescing.

"I s'pose you're balmy on her," he said resignedly at the end, "like what folks are in books. I want 'em with long tails, mind."

William was not unacquainted with the tender passion. He had been to the pictures. He had read books. He had seen his elder brother Robert pass several times through every stage of the consuming fever. He had himself decided in moments of deep emotion to marry the little girl next door as soon as he should reach manhood's estate. He was willing to further his new friend's suit by every legitimate means, but he was rather aghast at the means suggested. Still—white rats were white rats.

The next morning William assumed his expression of shining virtue—the expression he reserved for special occasions.

"You goin' shoppin' this mornin'?" he inquired politely of Ethel.

"You know I am," said Ethel shortly.

144

"Shall I come with you to carry parcels an' things?" said William unctuously.

Ethel looked at him with sudden suspicion.

"What do you want?" she said. "I'm not going to buy you anything."

William looked pained.

"I don't want anything," he said. "I jus' want to *help* you, that's all. I jus' want to carry your parcels for you. I—I jus' don't want you to get tired, that's all."

"All right." Ethel was still suspicious. "You can come and you can carry parcels, but you won't get a penny out of me."

They walked down together to the shops, and William meekly allowed himself to be laden with many parcels. Ethel's grim suspicion passed into bewilderment as he passed toyshop after toyshop without a glance. In imagination he was already teaching complicated tricks to a pair of white rats.

"It's—it's awfully decent of you, William," said Ethel at last, almost persuaded that she had misjudged William for the greater part of his life. "Do you feel all right? I mean, you don't feel ill or anything, do you?"

"No," he said absently, then corrected himself hastily. "At least, not *jus'* now. I feel all right jus' *now*. I feel as if I might not feel all right soon, but I don't know."

Ethel looked anxious.

"Let's get home quickly. What have you been eating?"

"Nothing," said William indignantly. "It's not that sort of not well. It's quite diff'rent."

"What sort is it?"

"It's nuffin'—not jus' now. I'm all right jus' now."

They walked in silence till they had left the main road behind and had turned off to the long country road that led to William's house. Then, slowly and deliberately, still clasping his burden of parcels, William sat down on the ground.

"I can't walk any more, Ethel," he said, turning his

145

healthy countenance up to her. "I'm took ill sudden."

She looked down at him impatiently.

"Don't be absurd, William," she said. "Get up."

"I'm not absurd," he said firmly. "I'm took ill."

"Where do you feel ill?"

"All over," he said guardedly.

"Does your ankle hurt?"

"Yes—an' my knees an' all up me. I jus' can't walk. I'm took too ill to walk."

She looked round anxiously.

"Oh, what *are* we going to do? It's a quarter of a mile home!"

At that moment there appeared the figure of a tall young man. He drew nearer and raised his hat.

"Anything wrong, Miss Brown?" he said, blushing deeply.

"Just *look* at William!" said Ethel, pointing dramatically at the small figure seated comfortably in the dust of the road. "He says he can't walk, and goodness knows what we're going to do."

The young man bent over William, but avoided meeting his eyes.

"You feeling ill, my little man?" he said cheerfully.

"Huh!" snorted William. "That's a nice thing for *you* to ask when you know you told me—"

The young man coughed long and loud.

"All right," he said hastily. "Well, let's see what we can do. Could you get on my back, and then I can carry you home? Give me your parcels. That's right. No, Miss Brown. I *insist* on carrying the parcels. I couldn't *dream* of allowing you—well, if you're *sure* you'd rather. Leave me the big ones, anyway. Now, William, are we ready?"

William clung on behind, nothing loath, and they set off rather slowly down the road. Ethel was overcome with gratitude.

"It *is* kind of you, Mr. French. I don't know what we should have done without you. I do hope he's not fearfully heavy, and I do hope he's not beginning anything infectious. Do let me take the other parcels. Won't you, really? Mother *will* be grateful to you. It's such a strange thing, isn't it? I've never heard of such a thing before. I've always thought William was so strong. I hope it's not consumption or anything like that. How does consumption begin?"

Mr. French had had no conception of the average weight of a sturdy, small boy of eleven. He stumbled along unsteadily.

"Oh, no," he panted. "Don't mention it—don't mention it. It's a pleasure—really it is. No, indeed you mustn't take the parcels. You have quite enough already. Quite enough. No, he isn't a bit heavy. Not a bit. I'm so glad I happened to come by at a moment that I could do you a service. *So* glad!" He paused to mop his brow. He was breathing very heavily. There was a violent and quite unreasonable hatred of William at his heart.

"Don't you think you could walk now—just a bit, William?" he said, with a touch of exasperation in his panting voice. "I'll help you walk."

"All right," William acceded readily. "I don't mind. I'll lean on you hard, shall I?"

"Do you feel well enough?" said Ethel anxiously.

"Oh, yes. I can walk now, if he wants—I mean if he doesn't mind me holding on to his arm. I feel as if I was goin' to be *quite* all right soon. I'm nearly all right now."

The three of them walked slowly up the drive to the Browns' house, William leaning heavily on the young man's arm. Mrs. Brown saw them from the window and ran to the door.

"Oh, dear!" she said. "You've run over him on your motor-cycle. I knew you'd run over somebody soon. I said when I saw you passing on it yesterday—"

Ethel interrupted indignantly.

"Why, Mother, Mr. French has been so kind. I can't think what I'd have done without him. William was taken ill and couldn't walk, and Mr. French has carried him all the way from the other end of the road, on his back."

"Oh, I'm *so* sorry! How very kind of you, Mr. French. Do come in and stay to lunch. William, go upstairs to bed at once and I'll ring up Dr. Ware."

"No," said William firmly. "Don't bother poor Dr. Ware. I'm all right now. Honest I am. He'd be mad to come and find me all right."

"Of course you must see a doctor."

"No, I *mustn't.* You don't understand. It wasn't that kind of not-wellness. A doctor couldn't of done me no good. I jus'—jus' came over queer," he ended, remembering a phrase he had heard used recently by the charwoman.

"What do you think, Mr. French?" said Mrs. Brown anxiously.

Both Mrs. Brown and Ethel turned to him as to an oracle. He looked from one to the other and a deep flush of guilt overspread his countenance.

"Oh—er—well," he said nervously. "He *looks* all right, doesn't he? I—er—wouldn't bother. Just—er—don't worry him with questions. Just—let him go about as usual. I—er—think it's best to—let him forget it," he ended weakly.

"Of course, he's growing very fast."

"Yes. I expect it was just a sort of growing weakness," said Mr. French brightly.

"But Mr. French was *splendid!*" said Ethel enthusiastically, "simply splendid. William, I don't think you realise how kind it was of Mr. French. I think you ought to thank him."

William fixed his benefactor with a cold eye.

"Thank you very much indeed for carrying me," he said. Then, as his mother turned to Ethel with a remark about the lunch, he added, "*Two*, remember, and with long tails!"

Mr. French stayed for lunch and spent the afternoon golfing with Ethel up at the links. William was wrapped up in rugs and laid upon the drawing-room sofa after lunch and left to sleep off his mysterious complaint in quietness with the blinds down.

Mrs. Brown, entering on tiptoe to see how her son was faring, found him gone.

"Oh, he's gone," she said anxiously to her husband. "I left him so comfortable on the sofa, and told him to try to sleep. Sleep is so important when you're ill. And now he's gone—he'll probably stay away till bedtime!"

"All right," said her husband sardonically. "Be thankful for small mercies."

Ethel and her esquire returned to tea and, yielding to the entreaties of the family, who looked upon him as William's saviour, he stayed to dinner. He spent the evening playing inadequate accompaniments to Ethel's songs and ejaculating at intervals rapturous expressions of delight. It was evident that Ethel was flattered by his obvious admiration. He stayed till nearly eleven, and then, almost drunk with happiness, he took his leave while the family again thanked him profusely.

As he walked down the drive with a smile on his lips and, his mind flitting among the blissful memories of the evening an upper window was opened cautiously and a small head peeped out. Through the still air the words shot out—

"*Two*, mind, an' with long tails."

"Where did you get it from?" demanded Mr. Brown fiercely.

William pocketed his straying pet.

"A friend gave it me."

"*What* friend?"

"Mr. French. The man what carried me when I was took ill sudden. He gave me it. I di'n't know it was goin' to go into your slipper. I wun't of let it if I'd known. An' I di'n't know it was goin' to bite your toe. It di'n't mean to bite your toe. I 'spect it thought it was me givin' it sumthin' to eat. I expect—"

"Be *quiet*! What on earth did Mr. French give you the confounded thing for?"

"I dunno. I s'pect he jus' wanted to."

"He seems to have taken quite a fancy to William," said Mrs. Brown.

Ethel blushed faintly.

"He seems to have taken a spite against me," said Mr. Brown bitterly. "How many of the wretched pests have you got?"

"They're rats," corrected William. "White 'uns. I've only got two."

"Good Heavens! He's got *two*. Where's the other?"

"In the shed."

"Well, *keep* it there, do you hear? And this savage brute as well. Good Lord! My toe's nearly eaten off. They ought to wear muzzles; they've got rabies. Where's Jumble? He in the shed too?" hopefully.

"No. He dun't like 'em. But I'm tryin' to *teach* him to like 'em. I let 'em loose and let him look at 'em with me holdin' on to him."

"Yes, go on doing that," said Mr. Brown encouragingly. "Accidents sometimes happen."

That night William obeyed the letter of the law by keeping the rats in a box on his bedroom window-sill.

The household was roused in the early hours of the morning by piercing screams from Ethel's room. The more adventurous of the pair—named Rufus—had escaped rom the box and descended to Ethel's room by way o the creeper. Ethel awoke suddenly to find it seated on her pillow softly pawing her hair. The household, n their various sleeping attire, flocked to her room at the screams. Ethel was hysterical. They fed her on hot tea and biscuits to steady her nerves. "It was *horrible*!" she said. "It was pulling at my hair. It just sat there with its pink nose and long tail. It was perfectly *horrible*!"

"Where *is* the wretched animal?" said Mr. Brown, looking round with murder in his eyes.

"I've got it, Father," piped up William's young voice at the back of the crowd. "Ethel di'n't understand. It was playin' with her. It di'n't mean to frighten her. It—"

"I told you not to keep them in the house."

Mr. Brown in large pyjamas looked fiercely down at William in small pyjamas with the cause of all the tumult clasped lovingly to his breast. Ethel, in bed, continued to gasp weakly in the intervals of drinking tea.

"They weren't in the house," said William firmly. "They were outside the window. Right outside the window. Right on the sill. You can't call outside the window in the house, can you? I *put* it outside the house. I can't help it *comin'* inside the house when I'm asleep, can I?"

Mr. Brown eyed his son solemnly.

"The next time I catch either of those animals inside this house, William," he said slowly, "I'll wring its neck."

When Mr. French called the next afternoon, he felt that his popularity had declined.

"I can't think why you gave William such dreadful things," Ethel said weakly, lying on the sofa. "I feel quite upset. I've got such a headache and my nerves are a wreck absolutely."

Mr. French worked hard that afternoon and evening to regain his lost ground. He sat by the sofa and talked in low tones. He read aloud to her. He was sympathetic, penitent, humble and devoted. In spite of all his efforts, however, he felt that his old prestige was gone. He was no longer the Man Who Carried William Home. He was the Man Who Gave William the Rat. He felt that, in the eyes of the Brown household, he was solely responsible for Ethel's collapse. There was reproach even in the eyes of the housemaid who showed him out. In the drive he met William. William was holding a grimy, blood-stained handkerchief round his finger. There was reproach in William's eyes also. "It's bit me," he said indignantly. "One of those rats what you gave me's bit me."

"I'm awfully sorry," said Mr. French penitently. Then, with sudden spirit, "Well, you asked for rats, didn't you?"

"Yes," said William. "But not savage ones. I never asked for savage ones, did I? I di'n't ask for rats what would

151

scare Ethel and bite me, did I? I was jus' teaching it to dance on its hind legs an' holding up its front ones for it an' it went an' bit me."

Mr. French looked at him apprehensively.

"You—you'd better not—er—tell your mother or sister about your finger. I—I wouldn't like your sister to be upset any more."

"Don't you want me to let 'em know?"

"Er—no."

"Well, what'll you give me not to?" said William brazenly.

Mr. French plunged his hand into his pocket.

"I'll give you half-a-crown," he said.

William pocketed the coin.

"All right!" he said. "If I wash the blood off an' get my hands dirty nobody'll notice."

Things went well for several days after that. Mr. French arrived the next morning laden with flowers and grapes. The household unbent towards him. Ethel arranged a day's golfing with him. William spent a blissful day with his half-crown. There was a fair in full swing on the fair ground, and thither William and Jumble wended their way. William had eleven consecutive rides on the roundabout. He had made up his mind to have twelve but, much to his regret, had to relinquish the twelfth owing to certain unpleasant physical sensations. With a lordly air, he entered seven tents in succession and sat gazing in a silent intensity of rapture at the Strong Man, the Fat Woman, the India-rubber Jointed Boy, the Siamese Twins, the Human Eel, the Man-headed Elephant, and the Talking Monkey. In each tent he stayed, silent and enraptured, till ejected by the showman to make room for others who were anxious to feast their eyes upon the marvels. Having now completely recovered from the sensations caused by the roundabout, he purchased a large bag of popcorn and stood leaning against a tent-pole till he had consumed it. Then he purchased two sticks of nougat and with it drank two bottles of ginger-beer. The remaining fourpence was spent upon a large packet of a red sticky mixture called Canadian Delight.

Dusk was falling by this time and slowly, very slowly, William returned home. He firmly refused all food at supper. Mrs. Brown grew anxious.

"William, you don't look a bit well," she said. "You don't feel like you did the other day, do you?"

William met Mr. French's eye across the table and Mr. French blushed.

"No, not a bit like that," said William.

When pressed, he admitted having gone to the fair.

"Someone gave me half-a-crown," he excused himself plaintively. "I jus' had to go somewhere."

"It's perfectly absurd of people," said Mrs. Brown indignantly, "to give large sums of money to a boy of William's age. It always ends this way. People ought to know better."

As they passed out from the supper-table, William whispered hoarsely to Mr. French:

"It was the half-crown what you gave me."

"Don't tell them," whispered Mr. French desperately. "What'll you give me not to?"

Furtively Mr. French pressed a two-shilling piece into his hand.

Glorious vistas opened before William's eyes. He decided finally that Mr. French must join the family. Life then would be an endless succession of half-crowns and two-shilling pieces.

The next day was Sunday, and William went to the shed directly after breakfast to continue the teaching of Rufus, the dancing rat. Rufus was to be taught to dance: the other, now christened Cromwell, was to be taught to be friends with Jumble. So far this training had only reached the point of Cromwell's sitting motionless in the cage, while in front of it William violently restrained the enraged Jumble from murder. Still, William thought, if they looked at each other long enough, friendship would grow. So they looked at each other each day till William's arm ached. As yet friendship had not grown.

"William! It's time for church."

William groaned. That was the worst of Sunday. He was sure that with another half-hour's practice Rufus would dance and Cromwell would be friends with Jumble. He was a boy not to be daunted by circumstances. He put Rufus in his pocket and put the cage containing Cromwell on the top of a pile of boxes, leaving Jumble to continue the gaze of friendship from the floor.

He walked to church quietly and demurely behind his family, one hand clutching his prayer-book, the other in his pocket clasping Rufus. He hoped to be able to continue the training during the Litany. He was not disappointed. Ethel was on one side of him, and there was no one on the other. He knelt down devoutly, one hand shading his face, the other firmly holding Rufus's front paws as he walked it round and round on the floor. He grew more and more interested in its progress.

"Tell William to kneel up and not to fidget," Mrs. Brown passed down via Ethel.

William gave her a virulent glance as he received the message and, turning his back on her, continued the dancing lesson.

The Litany passed more quickly than he ever remembered its doing before. He replaced the rat in his pocket as they rose for the hymn. It was during the hymn that the catastrophe occurred.

The Browns occupied the front seat of the church. While the second verse was being sung, the congregation was electrified by the sight of a small, long-tailed white creature appearing suddenly upon Mr. Brown's shoulder. Ethel's scream almost drowned the organ. Mr. Brown put up his hand and the intruder jumped upon his head and stood there for a second, digging his claws into his victim's scalp. Mr. Brown turned upon his son a purple face that promised future vengeance. The choir turned fascinated eyes upon it, and the hymn died away. William's face was a mask of horror. Rufus next appeared running along the rim of the pulpit. There was a sudden unceremonial exit of most of the female portion of the congregation. The clergyman grew pale as Rufus approached and slid up his reading-desk. A choir-boy quickly grabbed it and retired into the vestry, and thence home before his right to its possession could be questioned. William found his voice.

"He's took it," he said in a sibilant whisper. "It's mine! He took it!"

"*Sh!*" said Ethel.

"It's mine," persisted William. "It's what Mr. French give me for being took ill that day, you know."

"What?" said Ethel, leaning towards him.

The hymn was in full swing again now.

"He gave it me for being took ill so's he could come and carry me home 'cause he was gone on you an' it's mine an' that boy's took it an' it was jus' gettin' to dance an'—"

"*Sh!*" hissed Mr. Brown violently.

"I shall never again look anyone in the face again," lamented Mrs. Brown on the way home. "I think *everyone* was in church! And the way Ethel screamed! It was *awful*! I shall dream of it for nights. William, I don't know how you *could*!"

"Well, it's mine," said William. "That boy'd no business to take it. It was gettin' to know *me*. I di'n't *mean* it to get loose, an' get on Father's head an' scare folks. I di'n't mean it to. I meant it to be quiet and stay in my pocket. It's mine, anyway, an' that boy took it."

"It's not yours any more, my son," said Mr. Brown firmly.

Ethel walked along with lips tightly shut.

In the distance, walking towards them, was a tall, jaunty figure. It was Mr. French, who, ignorant of what had happened, was coming gaily on to meet them returning from church. He was smiling as he came, secure in his reception, composing airy compliments in his mind. As

Ethel came on he raised his hat with a flourish and beamed at her effusively. Ethel walked past him, without a glance and with head high, leaving him, aghast and despairing, staring after her down the road. He never saw Mr. and Mrs. Brown. William realised the situation. The future half-crowns and two-shilling pieces seemed to vanish away. He protested vehemently.

"Ethel, don't get mad at Mr. French. He di'n't mean anything! He only wanted to do sumthin' for you 'cause he was mad on you."

"It's *horrible*!" said Ethel. "First you bringing that dreadful animal to church, and then I find that he's deceived me and you helped him. I hope Father takes the other one away."

"He won't," said William. "He never said anything about that. The other's learnin' to be friends with Jumble in the shed. I say, Ethel, don't be mad at Mr. French. He—"

"Oh, don't *talk* about him," said Ethel angrily.

William, who was something of a philosopher, accepted failure, and the loss of any riches a future allied with Mr. French might have brought him.

"All right!" he said. "Well, I've got the other one left, anyway."

They entered the drive and began to walk up to the front door. From the bushes came a scampering and breaking of twigs as Jumble dashed out to greet his master. His demeanour held more than ordinary pleasure: it expressed pride and triumph. At his master's feet he laid his proud offering—the mangled remains of Cromwell.

William gasped.

"Oh, William!" said Ethel, "I'm so *sorry*."

William assumed an expression of proud, restrained sorrow.

"All right!" he said generously. "It's not your fault really. An' it's not Jumble's fault. P'r'aps he thought it was what I was tryin' to teach him to do. It's jus' no one's fault. We'll have to bury it." His spirits rose. "I'll do the reel buryin' service out of the Prayer Book."

He stood still gazing mournfully down at what was left of Jumble's friend. Jumble stood by it, proud and pleased, looking up with his head on one side and his tail wagging. Sadly William reviewed the downfall of his hopes. Gone was Mr. French and all he stood for. Gone was Rufus. Gone was Cromwell. He put his hand into his pocket and it came in contact with the two-shilling piece.

"Well," he said slowly and philosophically, "I've got *that* left anyway."

*Have you read
the other*

WILLIAM

*books published
by Armada?*

There is no other boy in fiction quite like William. Richmal Crompton's stories about him have been popular since the 1920's – and he's still a hero of readers today. There are scores more of his hilarious adventures in these Armada books. Have you got them all?

**JUST—WILLIAM
WILLIAM—THE BOLD
WILLIAM'S HAPPY DAYS
WILLIAM'S CROWDED HOURS
WILLIAM—THE BAD
WILLIAM—THE DETECTIVE**

And watch out for more **WILLIAM** books in Armada!

has a whole shipload
of exciting books for you

Armadas are chosen by children all over the world. They're designed to fit your pocket, and your pocket money too. They're colourful, gay, and there are hundreds of titles to choose from. Armada has something for everyone:

Mystery and adventure series to collect, with favourite characters and authors – like Alfred Hitchcock and The Three Investigators. The Hardy Boys. Young detective Nancy Drew. The intrepid Lone Piners. Biggles. The rascally William – and others.

Hair-raising spinechillers – ghost, monster and science fiction stories. Super craft books. Fascinating quiz and puzzle books. Lots of hilarious fun books. Many famous children's stories. Thrilling pony adventures. Popular school stories – and many more exciting titles which will all look wonderful on your bookshelf.

You can build up your own Armada collection – and new Armadas are published every month, so look out for the latest additions to the Captain's cargo.

If you'd like a complete, up-to-date list of Armada books, send a stamped, self-addressed envelope to:

Armada Books,
14 St James's Place,
London SW1A 1PF